Not Giving Up On Forever

Yana Stevelork

Ukiyoto Publishing

All global publishing rights are held by

Ukiyoto Publishing

Published in 2022

Content Copyright © Yana Stevelork

ISBN 9789360162238

All rights reserved.

No part of this publication may be reproduced, transmitted, or stored in a retrieval system, in any form by any means, electronic, mechanical, photocopying, recording or otherwise, without the prior permission of the publisher.

The moral rights of the author have been asserted.

This is a work of fiction. Names, characters, businesses, places, events, locales, and incidents are either the products of the author's imagination or used in a fictitious manner. Any resemblance to actual persons, living or dead, or actual events is purely coincidental.

This book is sold subject to the condition that it shall not by way of trade or otherwise, be lent, resold, hired out or otherwise circulated, without the publisher's prior consent, in any form of binding or cover other than that in which it is published.

www.ukiyoto.com

All my stories are always devoted to you, D...

CONTENTS

Chapter 1	1
Chapter 2	3
Chapter 3	5
Chapter 4	7
Chapter 5	8
Chapter 6	11
Chapter 7	13
Chapter 8	15
Chapter 9	17
Chapter 10	18
Chapter 11	19
Chapter 12	22
Chapter 13	23
Chapter 14	25
Chapter 15	27
Chapter 16	29
Chapter 17	32
Chapter 18	34
Chapter 19	37
Chapter 20	40
Chapter 21	43
Chapter 22	45
Chapter 23	48
Chapter 24	51
Chapter 25	53
Chapter 26	56
Chapter 27	58
Chapter 28	60

Chapter 29	62
Chapter 30	64
Chapter 31	68
Chapter 32	71
Chapter 33	74
Chapter 34	76
Chapter 35	79
Chapter 36	81
Chapter 37	84
Chapter 38	85
Chapter 39	87
Chapter 40	88
Chapter 41	91
Chapter 42	95
Chapter 43	97
Chapter 44	99
Chapter 45	102
Chapter 46	104
Chapter 47	106
Chapter 48	108
Chapter 49(A)	111
Chapter 50	115
Chapter 51	117
Chapter 52	119
Chapter 53	123
Chapter 54	126
Chapter 55	128
Chapter 56	130
Chapter 57	132
Chapter 58	136

Chapter 59	138
Chapter 60	141
Chapter 61	143
Chapter 62	144
Chapter 63	147
Chapter 64	149
Chapter 65	151
Chapter 66	153
Chapter 67	158
Chapter 68	161
Chapter 69	163
Chapter 70	165
Chapter 71	167
Chapter 72	170
Chapter 73	173
Chapter 74	176
Chapter 75	179
Chapter 76	181
Chapter 77	182
Chapter 78	185
Chapter 79	187
Chapter 80	191
Chapter 81	192
Chapter 82	194
Chapter 83	196
Chapter 84	199
Chapter 85	201
Chapter 86	204
Chapter 87	206
Chapter 88	209

Chapter 89	212
Chapter 90	215
Chapter 91	216
Chapter 92	218
Chapter 93	221
Chapter 94	222
Chapter 49(B)	223
About the Author	*227*

Chapter 1.

The first chapter, which is the last one as well.

What fine weather...

The wind hinted at the coming cold, but the September sun still brightly lit up the small British town with its beams. There was a pleasant wood smell in the air. The noise of the passing by people merged with full harmony of the events around. Birds chirped restlessly, calling for the arrangement of dwellings before the forthcoming cold weather. And the road was so...

"Anna!"

The male voice pulled the woman from oblivion. For a moment, she lost all train of thought and turned toward the voice, startled.

"The phone, Anna," the tall, handsome man specified, pointing to the device on the table.

"Huh? What do you mean?" Anna asked, still puzzled.

The young man grinned and observed his wife worriedly.

"Listen carefully, darling. Can you hear it? It is your phone ringing."

"My phone!" Anna rushed to pick it up. "Hello? Yes, Timmy! Ah, my son, forgive me. I got distracted and did not hear you calling."

She looked towards her husband. He grimaced, hinting that his wife was more cuckoo than a clock, for which he quickly received a light kick. He chuckled and began making tea.

"Of course...yes..." Anna was infinitely glad to hear the son's voice.

 It's been two weeks since Timmy was not at home because of the sports center's camp, and she was nervous about everything.

 "Do you eat well? Yes... Yes, I understand." She nodded and frowned. "And you have enough money, right? Enough for all the needs?"

Anna's partner burst out laughing. He fully imagined all answers that a bright Timmy reported robotically and recognized himself at that age when his mother worried about his everyday issues and struggles. He approached and embraced his wife, who went on scolding. Blocking her way, he shouted to the receiver, so Timmy could hear, "And no girlfriends over there, do you hear me?"

Anna scorned, but agreed.

"And no girlfriends!" she smirked, hearing her son's protests. "Well, darling, off you go. Thank you for paying me mind. I love you. Call at the slightest opportunity."

She finished the call and turned back to her beloved.

"Listen."

The husband looked inquiring.

"I am so, so happy." She pulled him into her arms and again looked in a window.

What fine weather...

Chapter 2.

"Anna! Anna! Anna! Come here, right now! Anna! How long shall I shout for ya!?"

Anna opened her eyes that filled up with tears straight away. *Please, not again. Again he calls me. What does this drunkard want from me now?*

"Anna!"

She hastily jumped up from a bed and ran to a house smoking room for the umpteenth time in the night. Her mother has been asleep already. She was unhealthy, and to wake her up for some help did not seem reasonable.

"What happened?" Anna asked timidly.

The old three sheets to the wind stepfather glanced at her hatefully. He instructed her to sit down near him.

"Should I shout for you all night?!"

"Sorry, I was asleep already. I did not hear you calling."

"Ah, you did not hear. When it is unnecessary, you hear every thang, and here ya jus' *did-not-hear*. Now, rush outside and get me some cigarettes. Come on, you waif!"

He gazed somewhere afar with a drunk look and moved the embers into the furnace with an iron stick.

"Where will I go so late at night!?"

"What night? Are you blind? Everywhere it is light!"

"Night in the streets!" she was afraid that the remark would piss him off entirely and shook with terror. "Look out the window, please. Late already, all shops are closed."

"Was I not clear enough?!" stepfather squeaked. "Now dress up and run to buy me my cigarettes, or you will regret it deeply. Go to the kitchen and take the money on the shelf! In a trice!"

Anna was panic-stricken. She had no idea where she would get him a cigarette at −30 degrees of cold outside, and time passed after midnight long ago. This winter was just ruthless, but even more brutal were the winter nights. The horror of the situation did not allow her to think things through. She ran up, took cash from the shelf, and hastily returned to a smoking room.

"Here, here is fifty," mumbled Anna and saw stepmonster sitting in front of the furnace with his eyes closed.

She stiffened. As incredible as it might seem, this magical falling asleep of the drunkard in a matter of seconds was just a gift from heaven. She tiptoed back to the kitchen and put the money back on the shelf.

Quietly, she returned to bed, trying to squeak the floorboards as little as possible. All her body shook with fear. She was afraid to close her eyes, but she knew that every hour of sleep before school counted as a real victory. She squinted and looked at her little alarm clock on the handmade bedside table. It showed 3:45 a.m.

Another two hours, and you must get up, grab your rucksack, and run to school, away from this tyrant. At least for a few lessons. Yes, and school is very far, which means two-three hours of quiet life until you get there.

Anna closed her eyes.

Why are ten-year-old girls so helpless?

Chapter 3.

"What are you drawing over there?" Nina ran up and looked at the picture, which Anna was diligently painting on a large album sheet under carbon paper, trying to hold the original at a window together with a sketch. She was painstakingly depicting the shadows of the map that the sunlight prompted.

"London," she answered without taking her eyes off the sketch.

"London!" echoed Nina, considering better. "Why would you, anyway! Did you redraw the London map? My, my!"

"I am in love with London!" Anna giggled. "As if you did not know that! I will go to London when the time comes and speak only Queen's English! I will see Big Ben and Trafalgar Square. I will feed birds there. Then I will come to look at Westminster Abbey and will walk London Bridge to and fro."

"Bah!" Nina grunted cheerfully. "Who has that on the mind! You and your English, though!"

Nina inspected Anna's room. Stacks of books devoted to the English language were everywhere—textbooks, anthologies, fiction. Notes and clippings everywhere. Posters of some western celebrities of which Nina also had never heard, Anna was such a fan. It was pure fun to look at her, trying to explain the meaning of fan-girling all these actors and performers.

She dreamed of far-away countries, speaking different languages, adventures, and finding her Prince Charming. All this was a mere pinch of life to Nina, who saw happiness on more of an elemental level. Her routine of life favored being surrounded by circles of relatives and friends. Unlike Anna, she was indifferent to all these languages, movies, and books.

"Well! Who has the most beautiful London map?" Anna brought the girl back to the real world.

"Mm. You, deffo!" Nina burst out laughing and embraced the stepsister.

A pleasant female voice came from the kitchen.

"Mealtime, girls!"

It was Anna's mom. She looked up to her mother and entrusted her to all her secrets and dreams. Elena listened to her daughter's stories about how she'd go on long journeys, how she would make sure that her stepfather did not hurt them anymore, how she would become rich and all their debts would disappear, how she would fix mom's health problems and how everything would be perfect.

Elena always believed it would be so. Only for some reason, at nights, when no one could see her, tears flowed treacherously down her cheeks.

Chapter 4

And this was the routine of days, months, and years of Anna's school life. Humiliations and insults of the stepfather she perceived strangely, but endured them deeply and painfully.

When everything was heinous, Anna even felt some odd joy in the rare moments of peace in the house. The sobriety of her stepdad knocked her off the wagon. It felt right only when everything went ghastly.

She did not fancy school, but teaching as the process interested her. Realizing that she could not skip eleven years of school life's penal servitude, she perceived school as a haven from the solemn atmosphere at home.

She whiled away the boring minutes with drawing, composing poems, dreaming, or idly loitering alone because by virtue of or, rather say, by the weakness of character, she was very timid to make friends and acquaintances. It felt much better alone. Her imagination compensated for the feeling of being an outcast with the sweet maze of adventures in the worlds that existed only within the ethereal borders of her lonesome soul.

School days ended. Anna gathered the remaining strength, and in search of healing, moved to another city to study.

But what was ahead frightened her even more than the youthful sufferings left behind.

Chapter 5.

She didn't love him right away. During school years, she paid little attention to him. The only things she could recall of him at those times were his constant confrontation with everybody and slacking off.

It captivated her, just because deep inside, she felt the same fatigue and hatred towards the education system and considered herself a bird in a cage. But she lacked the courage for counter-actions or opportunities to respond to teachers' or schoolmates' offensive remarks.

She saw Mark again in Garth city when the university era of crazy twenties was in full swing. They suddenly got in touch with each other and set up a meeting.

Anna grew up a beautiful lady. She was slender, with burnished black hair and elegant facial features, walking through life without arrogance or anger. There was always a smile on her face, and her blue eyes were full of purity and thoughtfulness.

Mark's lifestyle struck Anna. A philosophy senior, he seemed so charming, so free. Appearance-wise, she did not fancy him at all, but it was that rare case when a person's inner world shone so brightly that it illuminated everything around. Involuntarily the beauty extended to the appearance.

Mark was not a yappy type, but often the enthusiasm or interesting topics loosened his tongue. He could narrate something for ages, even more striking Anna with his knowledge.

Mark was bright, though he did not realize it. He absorbed tons of information and would conquer the world if given an opportunity.

Their relationship developed gradually as they learned about each other, and none of the young people would rush things. It seemed, in such a quiet, measured development of events, without wild passion and absurd, was a sense of their relationship.

They went on long walks in any weather, discussing everything that two people of the opposite sex ever discuss.

All these trifles, all these meetings absorbed Anna until she was infatuated by this young man completely and irreversibly.

Where is this cross line? How can the feeling initially not designated between two persons arise just like that? Why does it contradict the theory of love at first sight, when based on an easy judgment about appearance, we can conclude that we are in love and that the person is "the one?"

Anna believed that it all starts with love at first sight, and not the one she experienced, the mature one, with rational conclusions that the person was right, his heart was kind and worthy of great love.

But no matter what Anna believed, this love has happened, and it was worthy of romantic opuses. It seemed impossible to love someone so deeply. It exhilarated her, and she was sure that she found him—her beloved for life.

Time passed both slowly and quickly. Their bond only got stronger over the years, making them look like older people living half a century in marriage—so strange and robust seemed their union. Life troubles couldn't strangle their feelings with its prickly branches.

Like all ladies, Anna was young and dramatic, often pointless to extremes, but Mark tolerated all her craziness with tranquility.

Anna found it necessary to test the durability of their relationship at each opportunity. Pursued by some literary ideals, she wanted to mold their relation accordingly. Mark himself was young and didn't understand the rationality of what was happening. Yet, he never let Anna drive them apart.

Mark graduated from university a year before his girlfriend and was on the verge of new beginnings. Ambitions and a craving to discover the world did not allow him to remain in Garth. He planned to move to the capital.

Mining Great City was the primary spot for young talents, dreamers of big money, and freedom that went with it. He could not admit to Anna that life in their town, with its cliché "born—studied—worked—died," caused him nausea. He madly wanted to share all his plans with her but foreknew that they cardinally dispersed in their vision of the future.

Anna saw happiness in small things. She wanted to be here in Garth, near Mark, get married, raise children, have a stable job, and a quiet existence, where they could enjoy each other's company.

That was what ended their relationship. Mark was endlessly angry that Anna vanished all ambitions, leaving only banal female prospects to have children and a cozy nest. Love changed her beyond recognition and broke the gap between them. Mark loved her, but his youth and his desires did not allow him to accept the girlfriend's views. He had to make a decision.

Chapter 6.

It was a dull, unfriendly day. The overcast sky threateningly looked through Garth citizens' windows, as if reminding them of the intention to change the mood at its discretion. Anna shivered and closed the window.

It was madly enjoyable to observe how the rain, as if forcing the trees to take a shower, drenched them with water tirelessly. Branches caved in underwater weight, wearily staring back at you, complaining of today's share of an unexpected thunderstorm.

Anna sighed, thinking about the pile of things that she had to do and the slush that would stand for several days, spoiling the walks.

"I am going to the capital." A calm voice came from behind.

Anna mechanically turned back and lit up. Mark. Gorgeous as he was, he stood in the door aisle. His expression was strange and suddenly frightened the girl away, but she said with a note of bewilderment in her voice,

"It is excellent, Mark! When?"

"In a week."

"For how long?"

"Forever."

It dumbfounded Anna. The reality of her lover's words stunned her even less than the look on his face when he mumbled the news. He remained quiet. She even felt he was glad. Confused, she wondered:

"Am I coming?"

Mark took her by hand and led her into the hall.

"No, you are staying, Anna," he muttered. "You only do not worry, all right? If we are meant to be together, we will be. You said that yourself before, didn't you?"

"Didn't I?" Anna echoed. Tears appeared in her eyes.

Mark hugged and kissed her. He talked incessantly about the destiny that they could again be together, that he would make a living, that he was suffocating here. He tried to explain everything, looked into her eyes, but she read only emptiness in them. It was as if she wasn't with him. The shock swallowed her up.

He was hurt and somber, but something inside him moved to all these words, actions, and reactions. All evening, he embraced and kissed her. But Her Majesty Destiny decreed that this time was the last which Mark and Anna spent together as a loving couple. It was not meant to be.

"I love you, Mark, and I wish you all the best," Anna said on the platform, seeing him off.

"And I love you too, dear Anna, and I hope for a future meeting. Let's be in touch, shall we?" Mark was anxious.

"Sure," she smiled.

Love is patient, love is kind. Is it?

Anna waved to Mark, who was smiling back.

"Sure," she repeated to herself under her breath and headed to the exit.

Chapter 7

"Annaaaaa! You coming or what? How long can you stay in the toilet?" Lara groaned reproachfully.

Anna giggled and, adjusting her make-up once again, hurried to the exit.

"Ready!" she reported to her friend, making a comic soldier's gesture.

Lara beamed and caught her by the arm. "I have so much to tell you!" she exclaimed, but the club music practically muffled her voice.

Girls rushed to the dance hall, asking each other every phrase on the move and endlessly exchanging friendly jokes.

It was a magnificent night. Dances till the morning. A flow of continually changing new acquaintances. Unintelligible, meaningless dialogues. Anna loved those nights when you could forget about studying, endless exams, work. Mark…

Anna shook her head as if trying to shake off the surging memories, but it did not help much.

"One more dance?" she called out to her friend.

"What?" all attention of Lara was occupied by the tall blonde lad. He was assuring her about his love, under his assumption, forever.

"I will dance again!" Anna shouted.

"Ah! Good! I'll be right here!"

"Okay!" Anna hurried to the dance floor, which was now for her a magic circle, where among the avant-garde sounds of contemporary electronic music, you could forget how bad you feel.

It was only one of a considerable number of revelry nights that became an obligatory part of the girl's new life rhythm. A peculiar method of suppressing obsessive, depressive states through dances and parties is a popular method among youth, effective and actual. Restoration through degradation. A universal solution all over the world.

You cannot forget, but you can ignore. It won't hurt you less, just as it won't hurt you more.

Chapter 8

Pip pip pip pip! the alarm clock would just not appease.

"Oh, no, not that, please!" Anna beseeched.

Her head was pounding, and though she never drank, the loud music, dancing, and impressions did not make her different from the most inveterate drunks in the morning. It was a sober hangover.

Anna tossed the phone on the floor, and it shattered into pieces.

"I warned you," she mumbled, looking towards the crashed parts of the device, but forced herself to get out of bed, feeling all the charm of terrible morning mood and the forthcoming study and work after it. The day promised to be intolerably long.

Anna sighed and began to dress lazily. She collected the phone in parts, confident that the device would still work fine, and wandered into the kitchen. The screen lit up, and one by one, the notifications of missed calls and messages flooded the screen.

Work took up all of Anna's time. She focused on her career, and only money was her motivation for any effort. All dreams of quiet family life, a bunch of kids, and a caring husband scattered like a fog, giving way to travel plans and purchasing material goods.

For herself, she decided that it would be, if not better, but more comfortable. She considered such a way of living an impenetrable shield, and the chances of ending up being hurt were close to zero.

She stopped filling her head with novels and focused on making money, not caring how much she had to earn—the process itself gave her a strange pleasure. There was something about it that showed confidence in the future. Friends and family could always ask her for financial support (often just using her, which still was unimportant), self-esteem from the munificent wages rose beyond the heavens. Nevertheless, Anna did not tell anyone about it. She just kept on toiling hard, and her success was proportionate to efforts.

She used to come back home late at night and, instead of rest, met friends, sometimes until the morning. It was not a correct distribution of time allocated to sleep, but Anna was sure that if she'd give vent to her inner introvert, she would spend all the evenings at home locked up, losing the last skills of socialization.

She always felt comfortable alone. People complaining about the lack of a soul mate caused her only irritation. She did not consider herself neither the "second half" of anyone nor needed "best" friends, understanding that one does not live on the island. People must communicate with each other by some unspoken rules and play all sorts of collective games like "boss-subordinate," "you and I are friends," "polite neighbors in the hood," "this is me, and this is me in social networks."

Deep down, she wanted to fall in love. To fall in love so that all this role-playing would make sense, that she was someone's if not second half, but the love of life at least. That there was this man, for whose sake all this worthless routine of life would make sense. But she always swept those thoughts away, trying to destroy them as soon as they appeared on the horizon of consciousness, until one day…

Chapter 9.

"Who is he??" Anna couldn't tear herself away from the picture of the guy in the news feed on her friend's PC.

"Who? Ah, that's Randall. My buddy," replied Puck without the slightest interest. "He just left. Lives in Italy."

"Left!" Anna could not camouflage her dismay. "He was here for a long time?"

"Yep, a few months. He is an excellent guy—religious, but without fanaticism, kind, and always ready to come to the rescue. He was everyone's favorite."

"No wonder" the girl sighed.

For many years, she did not meet anyone whose appearance could capture her that much. In the photos that Anna scrolled rapidly, Randall looked unreal—he was naturally striking, tall, tanned, and even in the pictures surrounded by ladies. His broad smile betrayed great charisma and openness of character.

He really was handsome. It was impossible to describe. Anna could not believe that they talked with the same people all this time but walked the same streets at different times but never met.

"What an eye-catching man!" Anna blurted out, not keeping her overwhelming admiration.

Puck chuckled.

"I knew you'd say that!" he shook her shoulder. "Add him as a friend. You won't regret it. Maybe one day he will come again, and you'd meet him. He travels often. This is his passion."

Anna reddened.

"Balderdash," she tried to parry but added, "I'll think about it."

Puck laughed again. He knew that his friend was already mentally writing Randall millions of messages.

Chapter 10

"To write or not to write—that is the question."

Anna looked thoughtlessly at her laptop's monitor, not daring to send a request to add to friends.

"Randall Parleo, Randall Parleo," she muttered feverishly. "Silly me! Randall Parleo. Randall Parleo."

Click.

A request was sent.

"Why did I do that?" the girl squeaked.

As she later believed, it was not just a request, but she wrote the lamest intro about who she was and what she wanted from him in the additional note.

"Randall, you're so adorable. I already love you and want a billion children from you" she tried to translate into the language of polite strangers as *"Hi, Randall, my name is Anna. I'm a friend of Puck's and accidentally saw your profile. Puck told so many amazing things about you. I just consider it an honor to get to know you."*

Anna gulped because it wasn't a minute later, the request was approved, and an introductory *"Hello"* with an emoji from Randall Parleo popped up.

She felt sick. Not from the fact that he responded so quickly and added her, but from how naively she began to think from the moment she saw his photo on the social network.

She knew this mind-numbing feeling of infatuation based on a physical attraction, and it did not please her. Prudent, usually calm, Anna reread the word "Hello" for the tenth time, believing that this short message connected her with the love of all her life.

Well.

"Hi! I am Anna!" she typed again.

With the love of all her life?...

Chapter 11

This new acquaintance surprised Randall, but interest in Anna immediately took over. They corresponded endlessly on numerous topics, and both enjoyed chatting.

He was even more charming than in the pictures. Polite messages, pertinent jokes, funny short videos he sent trying to show Milan to a girl. It was all so adorable and yet profound. Anna just couldn't believe that such an attractive, unique guy lived on the same planet as her.

Every day, she grew sadder that they were far apart and could not get to know each other in real life. Randall took it more optimistically, saying he would one day fly to her, or she would fly to see Italy.

Anna's changed. Her usual cold mood, set only for work, dissipated, and it was challenging to focus. The Italian occupied all her thoughts, and she checked her phone every few minutes, ignoring the fact that the notifications vibrated in case of messages.

Anna stretched out on the bed and got up to make some coffee. The phone rang. She answered mechanically, barely taking a breath:

"Randall?"

"Em… Hi, Anna."

The girl coughed.

"Mark! Hi, Mark. I didn't expect a call from you."

"That I noticed." The velvet voice in a tube laughed. "Randall, huh?"

"The acquaintance," Anna hurried to cover up. "Nonsense, nothing serious. What're you up to? It's been a while. About three months, to be exact. Three months and f…"

"Three months and four days, right." Mark giggled.

"Are you… counting?"

"Certainly. I miss you, Anna."

There was an awkward pause. Anna took control of the situation.

"How is the capital? How's your work?"

The second line rang. Randall. The girl shivered but focused on Mark's answer.

"Oh, everything is great! Did I mention they promoted me?"

He didn't.

"Congrats!" Anna's voice came out somehow fake, and she gulped.

"Thank you! Come for a visit?"

"What? A visit?" Anna choked on his words. "To you? Oh, no, I can't. I have work."

"Is there never a weekend? We'd have a wonderful time. I'd show you the whole Mining Great from start to finish."

"No, I made sure I never had a day off." Anna felt a sudden resentment. The memory of every day she'd gone to work to keep from thinking Mark had left her came flooding back.

"This can't be. You are a teacher. You will have an obligatory holiday. Come, Anna. I want to see you. You know nothing's changed. I still miss you… I"

"I already have plans for the upcoming holidays!" suddenly blurted out Anna, not understanding what she planned to say.

"Plans?" Mark didn't expect that answer. "What sort of plans?"

"I'm flying to Italy."

"Italy!"

"Yes, to see a friend. See Milan."

There was a silence Anna did not even notice. The swarm of her thoughts in the chorus asking, *What was that?* drowned everything out.

Why would she say that? No such plans existed, but a sudden desire to hurt Mark got over everything else.

"Oh" Mark finally reacted. "Well, that's too bad…"

Anna heard some pain in his response. Wasn't that what she wanted? Now she was sorry about what she said.

She wanted to see Mark. She really did. But the resentment of the way they broke up just kept her from breathing. It trampled on her pride every day, and even after she forced herself to be friends with Mark and communicate regularly, she didn't feel any better.

But it was different now. Only a new love could help let go of an old one. Anna remembered Randall's perfect features the last time she saw him on video chat, and suddenly she beamed. Or maybe it was not a ridiculous remark? Perhaps this was her upcoming holiday plan indeed.

"Yeah. Sorry. Maybe some other time we'll see each other."

"Sure." Mark's voice was low, and he hurried to finish the conversation. "Look, I have to go, okay? I was happy to chat. We'll text later, right?"

"Of course," Anna answered. "Bye!"

The girl threw the phone on the bed and walked over to the PC. On the screen, the messages from Randall were flashing. *"Are you busy?"* he asked.

"Now, yes, I am. But free on upcoming holidays and flying to you." Anna wrote and giggled, expecting his reaction.

It followed immediately with a series of surprising texts.

"What?"

"You serious?"

"When?"

"Wow! Anna, I'm so happy!"

"Anna!"

"Hey, are you there!"

Anna burst out laughing and hurried to explain to him that the idea had just occurred to her. Still, she determined to make it a reality, and all the last part of the evening, they talked about how amazing she would spend time with this handsome man in sunny Italy.

Chapter 12

All the last week before the holidays, Anna hated herself and was amazed at the same time. Inside her, fought both the common sense, literally screaming that to fly to another country for two weeks to a guy she never saw was not right and dangerous; and the conscience, adding on top that it was also somehow impudent and dishonorable.

Another two fought with them—the *adventurism*, considering that the idea was just excellent and would bring many new experiences; and *blind love*, which had little in common with anything sensible. But the latter was the real argument, which was the reason for the trip.

Anna felt a strange feeling of infatuation. It had little logic. She never met Randall in real life. She saw him in video chats, knew his manner of speaking, his tastes, and habits. In a short time of cyber-dating, they talked over absolutely everything.

Every morning she woke up from a short text message, *"Good morning, beauty,"* and finished the day with *"Goodnight, Anna, waiting for tomorrow's communication."* She devoted all her free time to Randall, and it felt like she had known him for many years.

Doubts and fears changed her mind about the upcoming trip several times a day, but still, every time she saw a message from Randall, she succumbed to the temptation to get to know him in real life, and her decision again became in favor of the trip.

Whatever it was, there came a day when it was necessary to hesitate to fly or not fly for the last time. Already with tickets bought and dozens of happy messages from Randall on her phone, Anna decided. She gathered her luggage and looked around the apartment again. Then she grabbed the documents from the table, hurried down to where the taxi was already expecting.

The flight was pleasant, but the subsequent events made Anna regret that she had arrived at all.

Chapter 13

"Come on, phone!" squeaked the girl, accompanied by a bunch of stares. "No communication at this airport! And the battery goes… off! Brilliant!"

Some kind of disaster. It's been three hours since she landed. All possible friends and relatives already met all passengers, taking the same flight with Anna, and here she was, standing on the departure board, trying in vain to find Randall in the crowd.

The despair began to creep on her. What if he wouldn't meet her? What if something terrible happened? Or did he just lie to her and not even considering meeting her at all? What if it was all a game?

Anna shook her head, trying to drive away from the ridiculous guesses, but fatigue, resentment, and panic began to overcome all. What must she do now? Fly back? Stay in a hotel? Some taxi drivers were continually trying to offer their service in Italian, actively gesticulating.

A few times, passersby approached, having seen that she began to cry. They must have asked if she was all right, but Anna could only guess, as she didn't know a single word of Italian.

The airport employee approached her and spoke in English, trying to find out what had happened and if she needed help. Anna's face lightened up, and she was ready to embrace him.

She stammered to explain that she was expecting a friend, but he didn't show up, that her phone was dead, that she did not know what to do and where to go, that she would be glad for any advice.

The young man listened carefully and offered to call her friend using his phone if she remembered the number.

"You're amazing!" Anna cried, wiping her tears. "Yes, I remember the number by heart."

"Dictate it," the guy smiled.

Anna uttered the number rapidly and stiffened, trying to read the emotions on Vizzo's face—so was written on the worker's badge—when he began to call.

After several rings, there was a resounding answer. Anna heard Randall's voice from afar and exhaled. Vizzo spoke loudly and emotionally in Italian, probably explaining the situation, and then just shook his head for some minutes. It was impossible to keep up whether he was nodding it in approval or censure.

When they finished talking, Anna blurted out:

"What did he say??"

The airport worker shook his head again.

"Your friend is late. He will be soon. He will arrive by train. I'll take you to the platform so you don't get lost."

"Late!" Anna didn't know if it was good news or bad. The delay of a few hours did not fit in her head.

He lost his smile and offered dryly:

"Let me take you to the platform where your… friend will find you when he arrives."

He turned ninety degrees and, making an inviting gesture to Anna, went towards the aero express trains. Anna hurried after him. What did Randall tell him?

He showed her where she could sit to see all the trains arriving and wished her all the best. She showered him with thanks, and he left abruptly.

Little did she know that she was to wait for two poignant hours more…

Chapter 14

Anna struggled to hold back her tears. How could he be so late? He knew the arrival time and promised to meet her and turn the next couple of weeks into a dream-come-true holiday. What has happened?

The platform was already deserted, and fatigue and grievance began to beat her. She looked around silently, not understanding the endless announcements from the loudspeaker. Train numbers and time changed endlessly on the board. Crowds of people came and went through the barrier, and again, the building was empty. And so on to the next train.

It's been four hours since she arrived, and here he was.

Anna saw him at once from the crowd.

Randall walked through the railing, stopped, and unfolded a giant poster that read:

"I'm so sorry, dear Anna. Randall Parleo welcomes you to Italy."

Anna stood up and froze. Tears came to her eyes again, and a smile of relief shone on her face. He came. Randall was finally here. Here he stood before her, regretting, and… he was so handsome!

Reality hit her with all its force. Randall was just any girl's dream. Tall, handsome, with tanned skin and a snow-white smile. His brown eyes sparkled with happiness. Tousled bangs fell over his eyes, and he tried in vain to bring his uncomfortable but super stylish haircut in order. He was like a model from some billboard that you often stare at in the city. He radiated confidence and friendliness. Everything was ideal here—from his clothes to Randall himself.

Anna approached him and felt how all the resentment and fatigue from all hours of expectation dissolved as she looked into the lad's eyes.

"Sorry, I'm so late," he muttered under his breath. "I got in trouble on the way."

"Hi. I'm Anna!" she joked, trying to evoke a smile.

It worked.

"Hello, Anna. I'm Randall," he replied with a smile and waved the poster before the girl again.

"Lovely gesture," Anna estimated and hinted at her readiness to leave. "Well, how long are you going to keep me in this place?"

"Oh, I'm so sorry!" he yelled and grabbed her luggage. "Come quickly! You must be exhausted! Of course, you are! Come on. We need a 15B train!"

They hurried to the platform, and Anna began to believe that Randall could really turn her next couple of weeks into a dream-come-true holiday.

Chapter 15

Their acquaintance met all of Anna's expectations. She could not take her eyes off Randall, who chatted incessantly about the most ordinary things, showed something of the sights and on the go, as he later admitted, making up historical facts about everything. He had a charming voice and a thick American accent. Anna was afraid that the sound of his voice would be the most pleasant sound she knew.

There was something about him, some mysterious charisma, that seemed to brighten everything around. Even passers-by smiled when they saw him. Four people tried to make acquaintance with them throughout a quick way to the abode where Randall planned to settle Anna. He was so outgoing and gregarious that it confused and usually struck shy Anna.

"We're home!" he blurted out, approaching a small lodge in Baroque style.

"I'll live here?" Anna asked, gazing at the house with a smile on her face. She liked the idea.

"*We'll* live here," corrected Randall with a grimace, waiting for a reaction.

When it followed, he hurried to clarify:

"I'll sleep on the floor and never touch you."

"Oh, if you knew how glad I would be if you did!" Anna giggled at her thoughts but said aloud: "Dope!"

They went inside. The decor was marvelous. The unpretentious furniture had various art objects—an Eastern mosaic on the walls and floor, high floor vases with flowers in the corners. The windows did not have curtains, but bead pendants of fancy shapes and sizes played their role. The original tabletop with playing cards was in the center of the hall.

"What do you think?" Randall's voice broke her train of thought.

"Love it," she beamed. "Whose house is this? Yours?"

"My friend's," Randall explained.

Anna was a little puzzled by the answer. She figured Randall would let her stay at his place. It was a bit weird that he'd arranged for them to live together for a couple of weeks at a friend's house. It was somewhat illogical, but Anna thought he might have a good reason.

"Great place," she responded, touching different interior items as if getting acquainted with them.

"Need a snack. I'm sure you're starving, beautiful! I know a great cafe down the street. We will go there not directly but in a roundabout way so you can see the park. It's just the bomb."

"The bomb!" Anna laughed at his choice of words. "I do want to see it!"

"Then let's not waste a minute! Italy is waiting, muah!"

And they ran out of the house, driven by hunger and thirst for new experiences.

Chapter 16

The cafe was indeed close by, but the road the Italian took Anna was worth it. They walked through a charming landscape park called Sempione, and Anna learned that Randall lived in the historic part of Milan, where every stone was a landmark. He fervently narrated to her the details of this or that place, half composing descriptions that sounded so improbable that Anna could hardly restrain her laughter.

He was in an excellent mood and craved to know the girl. They coquettishly exchanged glances all the time and nudged each other for some jokes. Randall had the camera with him, so he kept shooting Anna, crying out the names of the places they were passing, as if giving her a command to stop and freeze for a memorable photo.

"Peace Arch!!" Randall shouted in the voice of a mad guide. "Built in 1807 by the great Napoleon himself!"

Anna raised an eyebrow.

"1807? Hard to believe."

"Shame on you, tourist! It is reliable information. I read it yesterday on Wikipedia!"

"I'll double-check!" she giggled.

Randall took her hand. Anna was pleasantly surprised and reciprocated. Noticing this, he smiled and squeezed her palm a few more times.

"Palazzo del Arte!" he exclaimed solemnly and added, not yet dissipating the impression, "Designed by Giovanni Muzio in 2018!"

Anna laughed.

"It's a brand new building indeed!"

Randall blushed and laughed, too.

"I meant the year 1018! Yes, yes!"

"Well, of course you did!"

All the way, he showed her picturesque places in the park, not letting go of her hand. Anna couldn't stop looking at him. She made sure he didn't see that she couldn't pull her eyes off him. He didn't seem to notice anyway, as well as views of numerous passing girls who shamelessly admired his appearance groaned and gasped, receiving his answering smile.

They reached an excellent cozy cafe, owned by a full gloomy Arab who preferred to follow everything in his restaurant from the far corner, so that was the best angle. Anna continually cowered under his intense unfriendly eyes, but Randall didn't seem to pay attention to anyone but her.

All his mind was full of Anna. He inquired if she was comfortable if she liked the food. He ordered for her his favorite dishes, which he mentioned so many times in their conversations online. He endlessly asked questions, trying to get to know her better.

The phone rang. Anna darted a glance at the screen, trying not to interrupt the story of Randall's school years, which he was telling her in detail, chewing a piece of chicken. Mark's number came up. Anna closed the phone screen with her hand. Her face showed embarrassment because Randall suddenly asked:

"Ex-boyfriend?"

Anna blushed.

"What? No, no, it's not! A colleague. Work issues," she began stammering. "I hate it when they don't give me a minute's rest, not even... when I take the rest!"

They laughed, and Randall, his mouth full of chicken again, continued the story. Anna swallowed, thinking of Mark. Why was she reacting like this? They were just friends, and she didn't have to answer him. Last few months, they had been talking desultorily, mostly because of Anna's growing resentment.

The more time passed since their breakup, the more she grew hurt by the unrelenting pain of the way he had broken up with her. She had to move on. If Mark loved her, he would have called for her long ago instead of inviting her over for vacation.

What did he want? Why was he even calling? To ruin her time with the handsome Italian? No, he couldn't do that! He better bounce!

Anna pressed *"Cancel Call"* and disconnected the phone. She looked up at Randal, who had once again answered the waitress with a loving look that no, thank you, they do not need anything and no, thank you, you can leave the menu on the table, as well as no, thank you, we will decide if we need anything.

Anna beamed. That waitress had no chance. "Randall is mine!" she whispered with a sneer, but it seemed that the wind carried it to the ears of the cafe worker, and she did not approach them anymore.

Chapter 17

"Anna, this is Bernardo. Bernardo, Anna," Randall introduced the girl to his best friend.

Anna smiled affably and shook hands with the modest guy with cheerfully disheveled hair and a sparkle in his eyes. He looked much younger than Randall, but his voice was shallow and creaky, which gave him several years as soon as he opened his mouth. And he'd been opening it, as she learned later, as often as Randall.

It's been two days since her arrival in Milan, and Randall had time to show her around. He did not break the earlier promised boundaries and slept on the floor, despite Anna's pleas to go to bed with her and separate the pillows if something embarrassed him, but he was adamant. It was a little hurting from a purely female point of view. Maybe I'm not his type after he saw me in reality? Perhaps he has a girlfriend? What's wrong with me that a single guy who stays in the same house with me for two weeks doesn't even want to touch me?

The hero himself interrupted her thoughts.

"I have a surprise for you, beautiful!"

She made a questioning face, trying to clarify that she wasn't a big fan of surprises. The young man waved his hand as if to ask for an explanation.

"You gonna like it. We're going to the Milan Mountains for a few days!"

"What?"

"Yes! Just a couple of hours by car, and we'll be living in paradise, baby! We will go up to the first peaks of the Alps' foothills and set up camp there. Just me, you, and Bernardo. What do you think?"

The last sentence was clearly messed up. Me, you, and Bernardo? Very romantic. Nobody has yet canceled the concept of a third wheel.

"Wow!" she exclaimed instead. "Great idea! When do we leave?"

Randall seemed to be over the moon about the girl's reaction.

"Now! Pack your things!"

Anna hugged him. She wanted to take every opportunity to be close to this charming guy who whispered in her ear: "You will be delighted with what I have prepared for you, beautiful. It's gonna be a hot night."

He smiled slyly and hugged her back even tighter.

There was a sudden crunch. Bernardo opened a pack of potato chips.

"Have no doubt." Anna rolled her eyes.

Chapter 18

The way they reached the mountains and settled surprised Anna a bit. Randall and Bernardo were always whispering and arguing about something as soon as it came to paying for travel, buying food, and camping supplies.

Anna suspected that the guys did not have enough cash for the trip and several times unsuccessfully tried to find out the situation. What made matters worse was that she had very little money left, having calculated everything wrong. Earlier she asked Randall to help her, and she would have paid him back indeed, but he was waving hands, telling her not to worry about money at all, that he had everything under control.

Still, every time Randall frowned about the money matters, she had a terrible sense of hopelessness and a desire to help that could not be fulfilled. Anna went on inquiring if everything was all right, to which she received a snorting "Enough, Anna, everything is under control." Still, Randall's and Bernardo's disgruntled faces overshadowed the whole trip.

"Why do we even need these mountains? I should have stayed in the house and just walk everywhere," she exhaled.

But seeing the Milan Mountains, Anna immediately understood why. They were unspeakably great. When they finally reached the place, her eyes witnessed the breathtaking scenery. The Bergamo Alps were lined with a vast number of paths that climbed to the top.

"Serio!" Bernardo shouted into Anna's ear and pointed to the waterfall in the distance.

"The highest waterfall in Europe, baby," Randall added, dropping the bags on the ground. "Ten thousand cubic meters of water falling, just imagine!"

Anna made a disbelieving gesture with her eyes and raised an eyebrow.

"For real!" Randall laughed, remembering what little credit he had as a guide. "And behind it is just a super valley called Maslana. You'll be thrilled. We will go there."

"Yeah, I love waterfalls," Bernardo muttered in the affirmative.

"Where are we even?" she asked admiringly, looking around.

"En route to Rifugio Curo," Randall explained. "You'll see. But first, we have to eat."

"Let's eat in the valley. I'm too lazy to cook," offered Bernardo with a drawling voice for the more remarkable confirmation of fatigue.

"Bernardo, I need to talk to you for a sec." Randall's smile faded. "Anna, just a minute."

Guys went off the grid. Anna sighed sadly. She was sure that the money matter had come up again. Surely to "eat in the valley" wasn't cheap since Randall got so down. Friends returned in a few minutes, and Anna did not expect mood swings—Randall was simply glowing.

"You can try the casoncelli in the valley. It's a local ravioli. You'll like it. And they make great polenta."

What a drastic change.

"Meaty! I love meaty!" Bernardo was also in a good mood.

"Meat?" Anna snorted. "I'm a vegetarian!"

The men froze. It was clear that they found some ingenious way to solve the financial conflict and were willing to fork out for the Bergamo lunch, and then Anna, with her gastronomic remark, destroyed everything.

"Oh," that's all Randall could get out.

"What is this *'vetarian'* thing?" Bernardo asked simply.

Anna could not help but notice the comical note of the whole situation and burst out laughing. Randall caught up, and they both, barely glancing at the calm Bernardo, who was waiting for clarification, again rolled up laughing until he frowned and said:

"So, I see you have fun. But my stomach is already cramping with hunger, so I advise you to start climbing into the valley."

Randall took Anna's arm and blurted out:

"Yes, of course we go. I'm starving, too."

He approached Anna's ear and whispered seductively: "We will think of something on the spot, for sure there will be a replacement for the meaty for the *'vetarians.'*"

He winked and kissed her, lightly tapping her lips. That shocked the girl, but again they laughed, leaping. Bernardo shrugged his shoulders.

Chapter 19

Anna's days have become like a fairy tale. She forgot about all the attainments of civilization—her phone went off on arrival in the mountains. The hut in which the company settled became her home for the next few days. A hot kettle, heated on the fire, was her shower, and fruits and vegetables, herbs, and spices were her favorite meals throughout the entire trip.

In Randall's presence, she recalled Mark much less often. It felt wrong to think of him. He surrounded her with such care that it was merely inappropriate to think of anyone else.

Altogether, they went swimming in the waterfall. Anna even grew fond of Bernardo, as she was learning more about him. It turned out that he was just an excellent cook. Every morning and evening, he cut, cooked, boiled, fried on the fire different goodies, and after he learned what vegetarianism was, he took this point into account in the menu with respect.

Anna still wanted to get private with Randall. Every time the situation became romantic, Bernardo seemed to smell it and appeared between them with an innocent face. For him, the idea that young people would like to be alone did not even exist in the galaxy.

And now, when Anna lost her mind and attacked Randall with a kiss, Bernardo cheerfully shouted behind:

"Some tea, guys!"

Randall barely separated from Anna's lips. His head swirled with such a sudden rush of passion, and he pulled her back to him. His plump lips were biting hers, and she passionately wrapped her hands around his neck, afraid to let go of the moment. Both were breathing heavily.

"Tea! Where you guys at?" Bernardo crawled along the cliff to the waterfall where the couple was.

They have disunited the bonds from the unexpected proximity of his voice.

"Come on, Bernie!" Randall swore, slamming his fists into the water. "Tea your grandmother, what do you want?"

"Some tea, guys!" Bernardo had not even heard of all this audacity in his address and finally got to them near. "I scream and scream! Are you deaf or wha'? What are you doin' here? Come, sister! Randy, some tea, go, Randy!"

'Sister' was how Bernardo addressed Anna after she cured him of stomach pain one day, and it touched him dearly. She called him *'brother,'* and both enjoyed the new status of a *'family union.'*

Only now, Anna wanted to hit *'brother'* in the face with a shovel for him, not seeing the bait that his company was superfluous.

"Some tea, right!" Randall kept getting out of the water.

Seeing how his 'intimate part' got hard after a kiss in the water, he abruptly covered himself with a towel. Anna giggled.

"Sorry about the kiss. I couldn't help myself." She looked down jokingly.

"I'll think about it!" he grimaced, trying to walk so that his reaction from below was invisible to others in the valley. And there were many tourists. Very many.

Randall rolled his eyes.

"Where's your tea, brother?" he clowned about.

"I'm not your brother," Bernardo replied, walking behind him. "I'm *Anna's* brother."

"Where's your vaunted tea? My throat's dry."

"From what?"

"I was singing!"

"What song?"

"The berries song, Bernie. About berries."

Anna burst out laughing.

"I don't know that song," she framed the guy.

"I don't know either," Bernardo confessed. "Sing it again!"

Randall coughed.

"Where the tea at? Don't torture my throat."

"Ta-da!" Bernardo was proud of himself. He pointed to a luxuriously covered tablecloth on the ground as they reached the top of the hill he led to. The company craving hot tea, honey, freshly baked cakes, and fruits, neatly cut into slices.

"Delight!" Anna was in raptures.

"Almost. Been. Recently," Randall muttered through his teeth and smiled. "And now the song about berries!"

And he sang some clumsy nonsense, in which every two seconds sounded *Berry, Berry*. Everyone laughed.

Chapter 20

It was a peaceful night with stars strewing the sky and frogs croaking in the distance. The mountains sank into the shadows, and the moon shone generously on their tops. Trees merged in incomprehensible cloud forms, staggering and swaying in the wind as if slowly approaching giants. Everything changed shape to something mysterious and opaque.

Anna shivered. Even sitting by the fire, she could not forget the pervasive cold of the night.

Randall joined her and, putting his arm around her waist, wondered:

"What are you thinking, beautiful?"

Anna gave him a charming smile.

"A bit of everything," she answered honestly.

"Homesick?"

"Not, really. It seems to me I could live forever in this paradise."

"You just imagine it." Randall cleared his throat. "Even on idle existence, the one needs money."

"Is that it?"

"Is that what?"

"The money. Every time there's a financial issue, you grow somber."

"Bosh," snorted the lad, drawing with a thread on the ashes from the fire. "I'm not gonna lie, my finances are tight, but it shouldn't worry you. That's not what I meant. I just explained that such vacations are just a self-deception. Life is a groundhog day, where you get up in the morning, make money to spend it in the evening on something, just to get up again in the morning and continue in the same spirit until you find yourself the same unfortunate partner. Together you'd make children teach them to do all the same, while you can safely earn money for a decent funeral or get a little rest, allowing children to earn for your funeral because they will know perfectly well how to do it. If you have not taught them; if not, they can always ask friends, or neighbors, or strangers, because we all live by the same pattern of this warped system."

"There's nothing you can do about it, Randall." Anna sighed.

"I hate money," he grunted back. "I guess it's mutual because I never have any. But still, I am tenacious of life."

"Is that why Bernardo's here?"

"What?"

"You invited him because it's easier to split the costs?"

"Oh, nah. Bernie had nowhere to go these couple of weeks—he rents his apartment to tourists through the 'Host Association Milan Tours.'"

"Host Association?"

"Yeah. It is a platform for young people. If you have your accommodation in a tourist area or close to the center, you can rent it to tourists, unlike other sites, where users are mostly young people, students, or the creative elite. The owner can stay in the house and rent, for example, just rooms, or can leave, if it is his property, and get much more money, as vacationers will be left to themselves, without the supervision of the owners of the apartments and they just love it, trust me. Bernardo rents out his dead mother's house in the center of Milan, so he's usually with me, and we share the money."

"My, my. The Host Association. Intriguing," Anna responded admiringly. "Now I know why he's with us on such a... private journey."

Randall raised an eyebrow playfully.

"Aah... Now we know why you're so evil! Not enough... privacy!"

"What? I'm not evil!" Anna pouted.

"Of course you are. You want me?"

"What??" she did not expect such an impertinent question.

"I'm kidding." Randall laughed as he touched her nose. "Didn't expect, did ya?"

"I do!" the girl barked. "Didn't expect, did ya?"

The next moment Randall was dragging her into the cabin, taking off both their clothes on the go.

Chapter 21

He covered her with kisses. Anna reacted to every impulse of his passion. When he pushed her to the ground and entered her, she lost her mind. All the surrounding sounds dissolved, and the only thing she could hear was the frantic pounding of his heart.

They were in such ecstasy that they became a single organism—moaning, writhing, wet with sweat. He changed the amplitude of movements sharply, craving time to try everything before the climax. He was in a hurry, and often Anna dug her nails into his back, making him moan with pleasure. He covered her mouth with his hand so that the screams would not wake either Bernardo or the German family in the tents nearby. But she couldn't help herself and screamed so loudly that all his attempts were in vain. Their sweet connection lasted a long time, and they both reached the peak of pleasure together.

"I love you!" Anna muttered at this very moment.

Randall collapsed beside her. His breathing was short, and his voice was hoarse. The perspiration covered his entire body, but even in the moonlight, his eyes were shining with satisfaction.

"I've been waiting for this," he muttered.

"Have you!" the girl grimaced. "You can't tell. It's hard to know if you even like me or not."

"Nonsense. Come over here." He pressed himself closer and pointed to her naked body. "How can you not like that?"

"I hope we didn't wake Bernardo and those Germans."

"Now his famous tea would come in very handy," Randall snapped.

"I agree!" Anna smiled and kissed him a few more times. "I'll go fill the kettle with water if the fire's still burning."

"Okay. Let's get dressed. Where are all the clothes?"

They both laughed.

"You took it off us on the way. If it doesn't have legs, we'll find it on the way back to the fire."

"Go." Randall made a snide face. "Let's start naked and work our way up."

And they went out of the tent. The stars winked at them as if indicating where to look for things torn off at the beginning of something very serious.

Chapter 22

"You're so hot!" Anna whispered for the hundredth time, leaning over Randall's ear, who was lying in the tent, talking animatedly with Bernardo about oil prices and the upcoming political mayoral elections.

"Thank you. So are you," he answered, embarrassed again. "So, what I mean is the elections are…"

She couldn't tear herself away from him. She thought she would never tire of these magnificent features, of this radiant smile and endless ridiculous topics that this handsome man liked to dwell on for hours. But still, after they had "it," Anna, like all the girls, could not help but go back in time and compare everything with Mark.

She thought of him only today, for the first time in days. She could not help compare the two men's manners, gestures, habits…

Mark… He was different. He wasn't inherent in empty talk and endless jokes. They could spend hours discussing profound philosophical concepts, applied sciences, axioms, and theorems. If he was joking, it was rare, to the point, elegant even. Though not a luxury, a smile was not a daily tool of communication with this guy.

His attitude toward money was also different. Mark did not idolize, but he respected money. He believed it was necessary to achieve happiness. Without money, one could not travel, maintain a family, raise children with dignity, and give them a proper education. It was needed to ensure comfort in all areas—health, personal and social life. Because he never despised the material side, seeking a prosperous life. A state of shortage made him angry, just as it did Randall, but this did not affect his relations with people—he always was kind and polite.

In a relationship, Mark was gentle in all areas, kind and laconic. He was an excellent listener when Anna told without silence, even on the most trivial themes, and never in life was rude to her.

Anna smiled at the memory. Where was he now? At work? Did he think of her?

"… so I'm definitely for Pitti!" she heard the scraps of phrases, Randall blurting out, obviously on the subject of the mayoral candidates.

"He's a donkey, your Pitti!" Bernardo retorted, chewing corn. "Four hooves and a tail! Only knows but promises! Hee-haw!"

"I'm tired of listening to you. You're just a stooge teapot!" Randall was joking. "Like your Spaghetti's better!"

"Spinetti! And yes, sir, he is! He will set this city on its feet, you'll see!" corn was flying in all directions from Bernardo's full mouth. He flushed and waved his hands in defense of his candidate.

Anna had fun looking at them. These dialogues were a must-see show. She no longer angered Bernardo's company. He was sort of completing the happiness. His English was a crazy mix of every accent globally, and it was hilarious to listen. They were like the invincible squad. She came and sat down beside Randall, her head resting on his shoulder. He turned to her and grunted:

"Dress up. We're leaving."

Anna was taken aback.

"What? You can't be serious. Elections topic made you that mad?"

"Collect things. We're going back to town today. I have a new plan."

"How? When did you come up with a new plan, and why am I only hearing this now!"

"You're hearing it now because I'm telling you now. My friend called me. He has a luxury villa downtown, and he's going away for a few days, asking me to look after it."

Anna blinked her eyes in bewilderment, but the words were clearly to her liking. "Aaand?"

"And we're going to 'look after' his luxurious nest, ride a yacht and make love all the time."

"Randall!" Anna covered his mouth with her hand, looking at Bernardo in horror.

His face didn't express any, even the slightest emotion. He just looked at Randall and Anna and ate corn. To understand his brain was impossible. The fact that Randall "revealed" them so unceremoniously was unacceptable, and she glared at him angrily, not taking his hands from his lips.

"Mmm, mmm! Mmm, mmm!" Randall continued to explain the details of the plan with his mouth closed.

She took her hand away from his mouth in displeasure.

"Here, so get ready."

She laughed. "You're impossible. Okay, just give me a few minutes."

And she went to pack for a new adventure. The villa… Mmm, mmm! Mmm, mmm! Sounded great!

Chapter 23

It was a real summer heat. The entire company, breathing heavily, wandered along the beach, searching for a saving canopy of some inexpensive cafe where you could buy ice cream or cold soda.

"Will he call anytime soon?" asked Bernardo irritably, exhausted from the heat.

"Stop it, Bernie, you don't have to be part of this trip at all unless you want to hold the candles when we…"

"Randall, how about this place?" Anna was happy to change the subject, seeing a cheap coffee shop ahead. "Let's see the menu prices?"

Randall was annoyed. They wasted three hours hanging on the Ligurian coast near Genoa, and his friend didn't call. On top of that, his phone was no longer available. Randall kept dialing the number that sent him straight to voice mail. His shirt was wet with sweat. He felt tired and angry.

"Randall," Anna called again. "Let's go to a cafe."

"What? Huh? No, Anna. We'll come there later. I need to reach Archie."

Bernardo cursed and separated himself from them. He lay down on the sand, ignoring the scorching sun and the hum of sunbathing tourists.

"Your Archie is the donkey, just like your under-mayor Pitti! And actually, you are as well!" he shouted to Randall, who pivoted and walked in his direction, clearly with the intention of physical violence.

"The only donkey here is you!" Randall cried out and fell on top of his friend.

"Randall!" Anna squealed and ran to separate them. "Randall, stop it. What kind of idiocy is that? He is not to blame! Enough!"

A pair of huge bodybuilders in bathing shorts in one movement separated two skinny guys fighting in a minute. Everywhere there was laughter and whispering. Randall and Bernardo tried in vain to continue the fight, but the goons threw them far apart, confirming that they were both indeed donkeys. Anna was full of thanks for the help, and then she ran to Randall and attacked him now with her fists.

"What's wrong with you!" screamed the girl, trying to return the blows to the guy's common sense. "Why do you always transmit your problems to others? Bernardo didn't deserve this. It's not his fault that your so-called friend turned off his phone and ignored you!"

"I know." Randall was breathing heavily. He looked toward his friend, who was standing in a group of some guys, probably explaining what had happened.

"Why don't we just go home? What's the point of hanging around the beach waiting for Archie? Maybe he won't call you back at all. Are we just going to stroll all day?"

"He'll answer. You just have to wait. He…"

"Delirium, Randall! I'm tired and hungry. I don't want to go to any villa anymore. I want to eat quietly and go to bed. This heat is simply unbearable. I don't understand why we've been walking around this beach with our luggage for hours!"

"We can't go home, Anna!" Randall bawled. "Okay?"

"Why not?"

"Because it's rented out. I needed the money to entertain you."

Anna was stunned by his manner of communication.

"Entertain me? Thank you very much, indeed."

Randall sighed and waved his hand dismissively. "Sorry, I didn't mean that."

"I think that's exactly what you meant."

"No. Listen. I thought the timing was perfect. While we are in the mountains, there are tourists from the 'Host Association' at my house. You remember that this is my buddy's house, and we would split the bill as we are all in one game. Archie promised to rent me his villa for a while. I don't understand what happened that he suddenly turned off the phone. I thought I'd give you a nice vacation at the bounty place."

"So there's no 'looking after the nest'…"

"Not exactly. Looking after, but for a fee. If you know what I mean."

Anna weighed down on the suitcase. She felt weary.

"What are we gonna do now?"

"I don't know," Randall confessed.

"Ah… Why cannot we…" Anna hesitated. "Why can't we go to your house? Not to a friend's, but yours? You have your place to live, right?"

Randall smiled.

"My house is very far away, Anna. I'm not from Italy. I'm just studying and working here. I'm Austrian."

"What?" Anna even got up from astonishment. Never had the question of his residency even flashed the girl. For some reason, she was sure that he was Italian.

"Oh."

"Oh?" Randall laughed. "Disappointed?"

"No. I just wasn't expecting it," she confessed.

Bernardo approached them. There was no trace of anger on his face. He put his arm around Anna and asked:

"What's decided?"

Randall rose and shook off the sand from his jeans.

"I don't know, Bernie," he hissed.

"I see. I'll be back." And Bernardo hastily withdrew, on the move dialing someone's phone number.

"I'm sorry, Anna. I know it's all a mess, and you're tired and hungry. Here you go. It's the last of the cash that remained. I'll find more later. Go to the cafe, buy something there."

"And you?" Anna took the money hesitantly.

"I'll wait right here. I'm dizzy," Randall replied calmly, kissing her hand.

She sighed and went to the coffee shop. It would be a hard day.

Chapter 24

And hard it was. The whole company, for a few hours more, has been loitering along and across the dam with boiled corn and potato chips in hands. Anna's fingers ached from the weight of the suitcase. The guys tried so hard to joke, but everyone knew that this couldn't go on like that anymore.

"Finally!" Bernardo cried out suddenly, pulling the ringing phone out of his pants and answering it.

"Who's that?" Anna asked in a whisper, not taking her eyes off the Italian-speaking Bernardo.

"Have no idea," Randall shrugged. He was all sweating.

After a few minutes of emotional conversation and endless 'Grazia, Grazia,' a cheered Bernardo turned to the guys and rattled:

"So, losers, I'll save you! We're going to Lecco. My friend knows another friend who has a lady friend who has a place for us to sleep!"

"What?" Randall frowned incredulously. "Do you know this lady friend?"

"No, Randy, but I know she has a place, and that's all I want to know right now. Come on. The bus is leaving in fifteen minutes. I would like not to miss it. Otherwise, we will be waiting for another two hours. Move on!"

"Following the instructions of Bernardo is in the highest degree uncomfortable," Anna giggled, obediently following Bernardo ahead of her.

"We go to our end," Randall joked.

They reached the station and found the right bus with no problems. There were almost no people, so they easily located immediately on several seats.

"Is Lecco a beautiful city?" Anna asked.

"It stands on the banks of Lake Como in the Bergamo Alps," Randall held out thoughtfully, looking off into the distance.

"What city in Austria are you from?"

"From the capital, Vienna. Do you know?"

"Of course I do," said Anna. "Will you take me there sometime?"

"And me?" Bernardo put in, his eyes falling in love.

"You're so ugly with that grimace!" Randall threw the bag at him.

Everyone laughed.

"You just don't love me, you callous fool!" Bernardo shouted, dodging the blows.

Anna clung to Randall and closed her eyes. Fatigue broke her. She was driving to an unknown place. It felt like she was some kind of hobo. She hadn't been in this situation before, but it was comforting to have Randall around. And yet, she thought back home. To a state of stability and constancy. A feeling that only... Mark gave her...

Chapter 25

"Mark?" Randall asked. "Who's Mark?"

"What?" the girl blinked blankly, trying to wake up.

"You called me Mark right now."

"What? No, that's ridiculous. I was asleep. I don't know who I was talking to. It was a dream. I wasn't talking to you."

Randall frowned. "I woke you, and you called me Mark."

"Me?... Randall, I just..."

"Come on, don't explain." He pushed her lightly on the shoulder. "Grab your bag. We're here."

It confused Anna. She could not remember the dream, but it was so awkward that she called Randall the name of her ex. Good thing he dropped the conversation. She didn't have a good excuse at the moment.

They got off the bus, and Lecco appeared before their eyes—the most picturesque city of Lombardy. It was located right on the lakeshore and looked like a fragment from a fairy tale. They stood admiring the Alps' magnificent foothills, Lake Como with its emerald water, and the surrounding resort towns' breathtaking landscapes.

"That way!" you could only envy Bernardo's energy.

He threw himself into the arms of a stout woman with a careworn face and spruced hair.

"Guys, it's Marla! Marla—guys!" Bernardo introduced. "She'll help us. Thanks, honey!" and he hugged and kissed the woman again.

"I thought he said he didn't know her personally," Anna whispered in Randall's ear.

"It's fine, beautiful. What are you saying?" He smiled. "I'll go hug Marla, too."

He wrapped his arms around Marla with the same enthusiasm, receiving them both with due attention, not surprised. That could not be said about Anna.

"And this is Anna, my friend," Randall said. "Anna, go give Marla a hug!"

"Me? What?" startled the girl, but Marla herself took the initiative and, continuously murmuring something sweet in Italian, embraced and kissed Anna all over her face.

They are all so... open-minded in Italy!

"Come on, come on!" said Marla, finally releasing Anna. "That's close place. Very close mi apartment! A nice caldo apartment to friends! Bene! Bene! Very good!"

They went to the house of a woman, telling the boys something briskly on the go. Anna understood nothing, so she simply preferred to look at nature.

They got to the place quickly, and in a few minutes, the hostess had already placed them on the couch and served tea.

She was a sturdy, beautiful woman in her thirties. Anna later learned that she was divorced and lived in this house with four children and two dogs. She made her living cleaning houses for rich people and sometimes hosted passing-by tourists. She did not take the company's money, saying that they were friends of her good friends, and from friends, she never took a dime.

After a festive get-together exclusively in Italian, Marla showed guests to separate rooms. Bernardo was placed in a large spacious hall with children and for Anna and Randall hostess, courteously not asking any additional questions, allocated space for guests, and retired to her bedroom.

As soon as Anna spotted the bed, she collapsed on it in exhaustion.

"Don't even think about it." Randall's voice came from behind. "We're going to have hot, incessant fun all night. Undress."

"You're out of your mind, Randall!" Anna hissed. "We were allowed to spend the night. It's not a motel for you, do not even thi..."

Her mouth was immediately covered with a kiss. She was about to have a hot, very hot end to the already hot day.

Chapter 26

"**My** legs hurt!" groaned Anna, failing to hide her satisfaction.

"Poor thing!" Randall sympathized, putting on his clothes and grinning.

They walked out of the room to the smell of baking. Marla, her children, and Bernardo had already settled at the kitchen table and, gobbling up the freshly baked bagels, discussed something animatedly. They smiled happily, seeing Anna and Randall awake, and invited them to the table.

The morning was in conversations about family, politics, and weather. Anna only smiled blankly and then left the company altogether, deciding that it was time to charge the phone and check the incoming mail finally.

As soon as the screen lit up, notifications flashed, and Anna grimaced. She was sure they were from students, their parents, or still anything work-related. She skimmed through the numerous letters, trying to pay attention to the most important ones, but an incoming call interrupted her work. *"Mark"* flashed the screen.

Anna doubted for a moment whether she should pick up.

"Hello!" she mumbled as cheerfully as she could.

"Anna!" a half-shout sounded in the receiver. "I almost went crazy! I bombarded your phone trying to reach you! You okay?"

"What's wrong, Mark? You know I'm on vacation in Italy. I told you."

"You just forgot to mention that you disconnect on vacation!"

"Mark, I..."

"Thank God, you're okay! How is vacation going? You're having such a good time. You don't think about me at all?"

"Of course, I remember about you," the girl replied in confusion. "But you're all right? Some strange reaction you have... I didn't think you cared if we were in touch or not."

"Wow!" Mark exhaled. "It is important to me, Anna. If you hadn't decided to go to Italy, I'd be holding you in my arms right now, apologizing for all the pain I've caused you."

Was that Mark on the phone?? What was going on!

"Mark. Are you drunk?"

"A little," came the reply. "But that means nothing. I'd say the same thing sober."

"Oh, right. Get some rest. I almost believed all that nonsense."

The tone of Mark changed instantly to hostile.

"Nonsense? Really! Do you think I don't feel anything? I waited for you. I wanted to make you my w… You know what…"

"Mark! I'm off!"

"Don't put the phone down! I love you! Come back to me, Anna!"

"You're drunk. Goodnight."

Anna abruptly pressed *"End Call."* Her heart was pounding wildly. Mark's voice was in her ears. The familiar pain pierced her with a seemingly new force. She ran out of the room right into Randall, who was walking towards her.

"Whoa, whoa, whoa, easy, pretty lady!" he exclaimed, picking up the girl as he walked. "What's your hurry?"

Anna looked into his eyes. She was shaking.

"What's wrong?" Randall got concerned when he saw her condition.

"I love you, Randall. You love me too, don't you?" Anna began to cry and clung to him.

He hugged her and held her tighter.

"Everything will be fine. Everything's going to be okay. Calm down, dear."

Chapter 27

"Can't believe it!" Bernardo shouted, looking at the phone screen.

"Huh?" Randall asked anxiously.

"Teo! This rich boy has taken all the tourists away from us again!"

"What?" Randall jumped up to a friend and gazed at his phone, reading something.

"Guys, what's the matter?" Anna asked blankly.

"I despise that arrogant guitarist!" cursed Randall, not hearing anything around.

"Randall!" Anna called in displeasure. "What's up!"

"What? Ah, Anna. We have a problem. Our competitor Teo stole our tourists! We had an agreement with 'em until January 15, but they already want to move out. And where do you think- to his mansion!"

"What makes you think that?"

"They just texted Bernardo that Teo offered them a free stay!"

"Why? What's his benefit?"

"He just wants to piss me off. He's got tons of money—he's a popular DJ—but he only joined "Milan Tours Host Association" to make me mad."

"Why would he?"

"The rich have their quirks. He wants to prove he's tougher than me."

"Are you friends?"

"No, and never will be. One random meeting, one completely random conversation about the "Host Association" made us competitors. No, that's just unthinkable! What a peasant!"

"Let's get back to Milan," Bernardo grunted.

"What?" Anna already started to think that these changes in scenery rarely lead to something good.

"Let's," Randall replied decisively. "Get ready, beautiful. Let's go thank benevolent-minded Marla for such a warm welcome and get out of here."

"Randall!"

"Do you have any other options?"

Anna sighed and shook her head negatively.

"Perfect. Waiting for you in the hall." He kissed the girl and left with Bernardo.

The whole company together thanked Marla, who was even sad about them leaving so soon and, turning towards the station, they took a road to Milan.

Chapter 28

Despite the long journey, Anna was happy to return to the old place from which it all began. The atmosphere immediately changed. Friends were always joking, and nothing seemed to overshadow the last days of her trip to Milan.

Randall, ignoring the tourists' problems, behaved still thoughtfully and courteously, tried to please the girl, showered her with kisses and compliments. Anna bathed in benevolence and did not want to even think about how she would need to return to Garth city in a couple of days.

"What happens then?" she asked as they both lay on the sofa, dangling their legs.

"What do you mean?" Randall, busy reading the news feed on his phone, asked blankly.

"What will happen to us, then?"

"Beauty, don't worry your head about anything. Just hold me tight." He kissed her on the lips and went back to reading.

Anna sighed heavily. She looked at him. So handsome, he perused the unimportant to Anna pages. Randall adored reading political news, controversies, debates, and various stand-up comedies. He could laugh for hours at different videos and always made Anna join him, who curled up near and listened to his ringing laughter.

But now, he read something more severe than the jokes because his forehead showed frown lines. Sometimes he would mutter to himself some paragraphs, messing his shiny hair.

Today he was wearing a wide white t-shirt and jeans, but this casual style only added to his charm. His tanned skin contrasted spectacularly with the material, and his jeans were a bit tight, giving enough to understand how tall and stately he was.

Anna smiled. Soon she wouldn't be able to look at Randall like that, immersed in reading. She clung to him and kissed him.

I love you, Randall Parleo... she thought to herself, but not a word was said aloud.

"I love you, Anna!" Bernardo's voice rang out.

She was taken aback. Bernardo flew into the room and, with a laugh, fell right on top of the couple.

"How about some tea?" he asked defiantly. "All set!"

Randall put the phone down and made a face.

"Some tea! Bern, your company is superfluous but sure! Who needs a personal life when you got tea! Come on, then! Bring up da cupsies!"

The guys laughed as he stood up and wandered into the kitchen, endlessly calling Anna. She looked at the flashing screen of Randall's phone. The temptation to check the device overshadowed all logical thinking, and Anna pressed the chat button.

The screen was flooded with flirty messages with hearts emojis from a ton of girls. None of the chats was read.

"Hey, Anna!" Randall shouted from the kitchen. "Where you at?"

Anna hastily closed the chat and shouted, "Coming!"

What did she expect to see? Why was she on the phone even? Did he talk to all these girls?

Her head was spinning from all these questions, but she obediently wandered into the kitchen.

Chapter 29

The last days of the trip flew fast, and now Anna was standing at the airport terminal, waiting for her plane. Randall held her hand tightly. And this time, they were alone.

Bernardo said goodbye to the girl the day before and left for some important business. Anna stood at the reception desk with watering eyes, and Randall was unceasingly wiping the treacherous falling tears from her face.

"It's not the end, is it?" she kept asking him.

"Don't be silly, Anna. It's gonna be okay. I'll see you again, and I'll make love to you again." He made a killer smirk.

"Will you come to my place?"

"Certainly. You promised to show me Garth."

"There's nothing to see there."

Her phone rang.

"It's mom, I better answer..." She hastily picked up the phone.

"Sure," Randall responded.

Anna stepped aside and reassured her mother for a long time that she was all right, that she had forgotten nothing anywhere, that the plane was not late, and that she would undoubtedly fly home safe and sound. Although Elena lived far away from Garth city, she still felt much calmer when her daughter was there and not somewhere in the world.

"I love you, Mom," Anna muttered. "Say hi to Nina, tell her I'm bringing you both a bunch of souvenirs."

She chatted with Elena for a couple more minutes and hung up. Randall was standing by, texting someone on the phone.

"Admirers?" It was a great moment to pick him for the "unpleasant discoveries" in his chats.

"Certainly," he said indifferently and hugged her. "I'm incredibly charming, right?"

"And modest," Anna confirmed.

"You're a fan of mine, too?"

"You wish," the girl winced. "Seems like you are more like a fan of mine."

"Here, I fully agree. This body is the most beautiful thing heaven has ever created, and I will die to have it again."

"Pff."

"What? Not romantic enough for your delicate ears?"

"*This* is only after wedding. Period."

"Um… What was it then?"

"What do you mean?"

"The incredibly long, passionate merge of our bodies all these days?"

"I don't recall any of that."

"Right. Okay then. After the wedding. This holds good."

"Great!" Anna laughed.

The loudspeaker announced the landing.

"You should go, beautiful." Randall gave her a deep and passionate kiss so that even airport visitors kept staring at the couple.

"Come to me, please."

"Promise. I'll save up the right amount and come straight to you, and we'll have a passionate f…"

Anna covered his mouth with a kiss. She was happy to taste his lips, to smell him, hold him, ruffling his hair.

She was afraid of the future, but now, kissing this handsome man, she was truly happy.

Chapter 30

"**W**here are you??" the stepfather roared.

"Coming!" Anna moaned, with shortness of breath from running.

"You're as slow as a turtle! Get ova here! Why do I always have to call you? Ah, here you are, finally. Tell me, why does your room look like a barn? What did you do? Hm? We know how to read books, but we never learned how to wave a broom, ya witch!"

"I'll clean it up," Anna muttered, lowering her head.

"Sure, you will! Otherwise, I'll throw you out in the streets. You like living there, huh? Like a dirty street cat, huh?"

"No."

"Huh? Can't hear you!"

"No, sir."

"Then grab a mop and a rag, and run to scrub. You pig! I'm ashamed to look at you. Straight A's, is called. Only books you can read, and can't keep no house clean. Pig, let me repeat. Shame on you!"

Anna moved toward the storeroom to get a bucket. Tears ran down her cheeks.

"Pig!" he kept on. "Filthy pig!"

Beep beep-beep!!!!!

Anna opened her eyes. The phone rang. She looked around frantically. Her whole shirt was soaked with nightmare sweat.

Beep beep-beep!!!!! The phone insisted.

"Hel-l-lo. Hello."

"Miss Ryans?"

"Yes, I am. Who is it?"

"My name is Millie. I'm HR of International School №678. We would like to offer you a splendid teaching position. I saw your resume online and certainly decided to call y…"

"Hold on, Millie. School? It is an old resume. I already stated on the first page that I am not in search. I'm already a successful teacher at the moment…"

"It's okay. We are ready to pay you three times more than you are now getting."

"What?"

"Our director is impressed by your linguistic abilities and is sure that you deserve a greater career and freedom. You will be very useful to us. I scheduled you for an interview tomorrow at 4:00 p.m. Suits you?"

"Millie, wait for a second…"

"How about 5:00 p.m.? Maybe 5-30 p.m.?"

"Millie."

"Come to the metro Bli Five by 5-00 p.m., write down the address…"

"Millie! Look, I… Wait, what? Metro? In the Garth there is none. Where are you calling from?"

"Uh… Mining Great, Ma'am."

"Millie, I'm in another city."

"Never mind."

"Excuse me?"

"We'll reschedule the interview for the end of the week. Enough to fly up here? How about Friday?"

"Millie, that's not serious."

On the other end of the line, a cute voice sharply became serious.

"I know you think it's very fast, Miss Ryans. But this is a great chance. You go out of the competition only on the achievements of your resume. The director, when she saw your file, put aside—or rather, threw in the trash—the CVs of nine candidates. You wrote the truth on your resume, didn't you?"

"Of course, I did!" such a question even hurt Anna.

"So you're on the verge of a big change, and me- on the promotion, which I advise you not to spoil. Metro Bli Five, 14 Rome street, building 6. Friday, 5:30 p.m. Waiting for you! Deal?"

Anna was speechless, but against her will, the answer itself came out loud and clear:

"See you then, Millie."

For a moment, she sat on the bed, blankly looking around the apartment. She landed only a few hours ago and immediately flopped down to sleep.

She quickly googled School 678, which resulted in one of the most prestigious schools in the capital. Millie was right—it was a chance for Anna. All of a sudden, she had a headache.

She scrolled down over the incoming messages, opened one, read it, and pressed the "Call" button.

"Yeah?" a man's voice answered at once.

"Mark, it's me. I'm flying to Mining Great."

"Anna? Hey. You what? When?"

"I have an interview on Friday."

"Are you moving to the capital?? When did you decide that??"

"Just now. If the interview goes well, can I stay with you for a while? I don't know my fate yet."

"Certainly. Wow, such a drastic change. You okay? How was the flight?"

"All is great."

"Mmm... Okay. So, wow, I'll see you. It is unexpected."

"You wanted to see me, right?"

"No, no, of course, I did. It's just so fast. I thought I needed to talk you into it for a few more years or so."

They both giggled.

"So, everything's okay?" asked Anna, herself little realizing the turn of events.

"There is no problem. I'll meet you at the airport on Friday."

"Thank you." Anna looked at her watch. "Nine o'clock. In the capital, the difference is three hours?"

"Yeah," Mark confirmed. "Anna. That's great news."

"Yeah… I guess!"

"Listen, I gotta go now. I'll call you later, okay?"

"Okay."

Anna hung up the phone and fell back on the bed. Her mind was swarming with thoughts: *Millie, work, Mark, capital, Randall.*

Randall!

Oh, indeed, it would be a dizzying change…

Chapter 31

The capital was a million times more beautiful and luxurious than Anna had imagined. Dazzling commercials, lights, posters with models, products, goods, and services urged you to consume and earn more to consume more. Only then would you be successful, and on your face would be a white smile that super toothpaste N. will provide. You would have an expensive suit from the brand M., a cool car from the brand O., and a bunch of fans offered by a promo company P.

But all this mass, all this fanatical materialism, and temporary illusions did not cause any negative emotions in Anna's heart.

We all think of the beautiful, living in this material web with its laws, and if not you, then them. She understood that. Having in mind only perfect intentions—to help the family, provide future children with a comfortable life—she played according to this cruel game's rules.

Therefore, the transition to a new level, symbolically denoted by moving from Garth to Mining Great fascinated her so much. She enthusiastically absorbed everything around, studied people, their submissive existence, expressed in amorphous movements, visible to the naked eye, or their daring strategies to bite off the "pie of success." She saw it in every detail, every passer-by, every conversation.

"So, how do you like it?" Mark wondered.

He had been staring at her for several minutes. She altered considerably, but in some ways, she was still the same. Just in what ways? Did she even have any feelings for him? He thought frantically about all this, trying to find the answer in the features of her face.

"I'm thrilled. This city is a game field for real professionals. I'm getting this job," Anna responded readily.

"What a spirit!" Mark admired. "You're not the same Anna that dreamed of a bunch of kids and worked crafts at home!"

"You noticed. This is a new Anna. The former died of a broken heart when instead of a bunch of children and needlework, she received the news that the love of her life dumped her, making it clear that money is cool and a career is a way to go. And this new Anna found out what is so cool about it, and now she fully agrees with him, and her heart no longer hurts—it is not there."

"Ouch. That was painful." The lad grimaced. "But it was possible to describe all somewhat… softer."

"As soft as it can be. Are we there yet?"

"We're here."

Mark's apartment was on the ninth floor of an old building. Anna hoped for more colorful views, but in fact, everything was grey and straightforward. The condo had a minimum of furniture and a maximum of cigarette roaches. The only place that clearly showed signs of any human activity was a computer desk. The rest was dominated by minimalism, created from desperation rather than design considerations.

"Beer?" Mark appeared in the doorway with two bottles in his hands.

"No, thanks, I am a total abstainer." The girl shook her head negatively.

"As before. Mmm, then… a pretzel?"

Anna laughed.

"Yes, perhaps a pretzel will do just fine now."

It broke the ice. For the rest of the evening, they bantered about all the possible things of any interest to both of them—medicine, philosophy, religion, pedagogy. Anna thought briefly that this conversation was so reminiscent of their everyday talks when they were a couple. Mark was sitting across from her again, giving out long scientific monologues. She laughed again and parried. Nothing seemed to change. It felt they were… together.

"Do you have a boyfriend?" Mark asked suddenly.

"What? Huh? Yes, I do. Or not. I don't know, to be honest. It's kind of vague. I don't understand it yet myself."

"Mmm. What's his name?"

"Randall."

"Randall," he repeated. "You love him?"

"Mark, what a question."

"You love him?"

"I don't want to answer that."

"Okay then, do you love me? Don't you love me anymore?"

"Mark, I think you've had enough beer for today. It is not the best conversation turn we have."

"*I* love you, though."

He stood up and approached Anna so that their eyes were facing each other. She could smell the alcohol from his half-open mouth. He gazed at her.

"Mark, I don't think the situation is developing in the right way."

"Anna, who do you love?"

"Mark, stop asking that."

"You're confused. Right? I betrayed you. You're hurting. You met him. And you want to love him. But you do not. Right?"

"Stop talking about all this!"

"You're fierce because I'm right."

He kissed her.

"How do you feel?" he kept kissing her.

"Stop! Mark, please, stop."

"And now? I won't. Study yourself, Anna. Study your emotions. Who do you love?" he was coming down.

"Please, stop!"

"And now, Anna? What do you feel now?"

He kissed her. She tried to resist, then gave up, then found strength again and fought until she gave up to his kissing.

"And now...? Anna...?" he whispered. "How do you feel? Do you still love me?"

He made calm, measured, but passionate movements, showering her with kisses.

But the truth was... She felt nothing.

Not-a-single-thing.

She closed her eyes and began to cry silently.

Chapter 32

"Coffee?" Mark entered the room with a tray and two cups. Anna had just opened her eyes and looked around lazily.

"Yes, would do the trick," she smiled modestly. "Been up long?"

"Yes, but you slept for, like, ages." He smiled back. "You have an interview soon."

"What? It can't be! How long did I sleep?"

"It's noon."

"Phew. Don't scare me. Plenty of time."

"Not that plenty. It's the capital. Everything is crazily far apart. To get to your school will take us about three hours."

"Three hours!" blurted out the girl. "I'll need to get a place closer to work, that's for sure!"

"What? Moving out so soon? I thought you liked me." He winked at her.

Anna coughed.

"You don't live close. And I only asked you for temporary help, just to get my bearings and shoot something decent, if the interview goes smoothly."

"It'll go perfect, Anna. They need a professional like you. We all know that. But even so, you can always live with me. I'll be only happy. I don't see the point in you spending money on rent if you have me."

"Thanks, Mark. But I…" Anna got lost, not knowing what words to pick to sound more polite.

Her phone rang. Anna looked at the screen, and her brain seemed to stop working for a moment. Randall. How to answer him? What to say?

"Answer it, Anna. I guess that's your boyfriend Randall…" Mark sighed, leaving the room.

Anna just stared at the flashing screen. The call was insistent and didn't seem to be the first one. She didn't understand what was happening to her. That Randall was her boyfriend never sounded the way she wanted it. She was afraid even to say out loud the idea that they were a couple. Not because she didn't wish that, but because Randall never even hinted at it. She had never seen him denoting an actual relationship between them and not just a holiday romance.

She wanted to hear with all her heart that she belonged to him, that he loved her, that they date, that nothing would ever destroy them. But he never determined such an outcome. Inside, she was torn by some dirty, incomprehensible feelings as if she had betrayed him, cheated on him, even when her mind tried to explain to her that she was single. Randall himself decided not to clarify the status of their relationship. But such arguments helped little.

"Hello?" she finally squeezed out.

"Anna! Finally, beautiful!" She heard a soft voice. "Where are you? I wrote and called. Wasted so much ink. Fingers hurt from typing. It's been days since you left me. Is that what you decided to do to me? Used me for a purpose and dumped me?"

They both laughed. His voice seemed so sweet, caring, charming. She fought back the tears.

"How are you, Randall?"

"Great! What about you?"

"I came to the capital, and I plan to get a job and move here."

"Wow! That's news! Anna, this is amazing! Congratulations, well done!"

"Thank you. So far, these are only plans. I thought I'd rent a place and invite you… You'd come, right?"

"Of course! I promised I would. I miss you so much, Anna."

"Me, too. You have no idea how much." She couldn't hold back her tears. "Randall, please come to me. I can't be alone without you."

"Hey, hey! What up with crying, beautiful? I'm here. I'm not missing, am I? I will come as soon as I can."

"When can you?"

"Do you want to see me in a month?"

"I do."

"Then it's settled."

"I love…"

The front door slammed shut.

Mark hurried out of the apartment.

Chapter 33

It was the fastest interview of her life. Without asking many questions, a kind school director just checked the diploma, awards, and documents and announced the terms of cooperation and remuneration.

Anna thought she had misheard it- the number of zeros in the salary was just too good to be true. With a boss attitude and making a half-satisfied grimace, she rolled her eyes as if wondering whether such a meager wage would suit her, and agreed. The director beamed, and they shook hands, parting until next week.

As soon as she left the building, Anna dialed Mark's number and shouted into the phone.

"I got it! I got a job!! I am staying in Mining!"

On the other end, she heard a satisfied chuckle.

"I'm so happy for you, really," said Mark. "It's a big step forward. Someday you'll be the headmaster of this very school."

"No brainer!" Anna laughed. "But I'm so happy! Now I need to find a place to live, since everything is going so well!"

"I already said you could live with me," Mark repeated and, clearing the throat, added, "if you like."

"Mark, thank you so much, but I don't want to be a burden. I'm eternally grateful for everything, but I want to live on my own."

"With him, you mean."

"What?"

"You will live with him."

"Mark, I meant…"

"Listen, I have a call on the second line. We'll talk later. Congratulations again."

He hung up. The smile faded from the girl's face. All the happiness was washed off in a second.

She knew that everything was going wrong, strange, but she didn't know what to do or how to stop it.

The occurred kissing scene both diligently tried to ignore as if the event didn't take place at all. Nothing more than that happened. Yet, ignoring the apparent tension made their communication complicated, unclear. Who are they? What was that? What for?

Anna understood nothing. Instead, she opened a chat message and wrote:

"We will always be together. You and me."

The message was marked *"Read."*

But Randall answered nothing.

Chapter 34

The answer from him came only a week later, and the events after that changed all of Anna's life upside down.

It was Tuesday—the day she would never forget once she tried. She had just finished her classes, and the endless cycle of working days, as often happened, alienated her from close contact with the people around her. It was the price of a career. When the focus shifts to money, the other spheres of life always suffer.

However, Anna tried from time to time to write to her mother and close friends a standard message asking about their life turmoil and, in turn, included a brief "report" about her own.

Randall, it would seem, gone for good, and if she weren't so busy, the offense would drown her. However, the days without their communication flew by rather quickly, leaving her with no chance to complain.

His casual *"Hello, beautiful"* came at noon. Anna read the message and smiled. Finally.

She dialed his number without hesitation. After a couple of beeps, his sweet voice already welcomed a girl so casually that it seemed they parted only yesterday.

"Where are you lost?" Anna half-joked.

"Oh, here and there!" Randall said, obviously chewing something. Anna immediately imagined him smiling and talking to her with his mouth full. "How are you doing?"

"It's all okay, just a lot of work. I've been given a lot of classes and a lot of tutoring, plus to that. And you?"

"Great! I'm in Garth-city!"

"You what?" Anna thought she had misheard.

"I'm in Garth!" Randall repeated and laughed. "Are you surprised? I came to teach. Puck didn't tell you?"

"He did not… He didn't say anything. How comes? Why didn't you say anything? How long have you been in Garth?"

"Why, only for a week!"

"A week?! You promised to come to me!"

"Hey! Easy, girl! And I will keep my promise! I won't be here long. I'll make some money and come to you. I said we'd meet together again, so we will. Calm down, beautiful!"

"Randall, I'm just unpleasantly surprised. You could have told me you were going to Garth. Why all the secrecy?"

"No secrecy. You're busy now. You've just started a new job in a new place. I didn't mean to upset you. You would start complaining that I'm going to the Garth and not directly to you. I need to earn green, and many people were waiting for me. I promised to come again."

"Many girls, you mean?"

Randall chuckled.

"Both boys and girls. What is the jealousy about?"

"Did you sleep with someone?"

"Em… Anna, why such a question!"

"Did you sleep with someone?"

"Anna!"

"Answer me, please!"

There was silence on the other end of the line.

"Oh, Randall, you did!" Anna finished the phrase in horror. "You did sleep with someone!"

"Uhm… Anna, you're acting weird. Yeah, I had some fun, but you—"

"Oh, my God!"

Anna felt herself losing balance. The impact was so strong that in her head, all clouded. Instead of the voice of Randal, continuing to say something, she heard only some hum. She had never fainted in her life, and now she seemed to look at herself from the side—weakened, falling to the floor, hot tears streaming down her cheeks without bringing her to senses.

"Anna? Anna?" was coming from a phone dropped on the floor.

Chapter 35

Anna came to her senses after a while. Her head hurt from the blow. She tried to get to her feet, but the body did not seem to listen. Reaching for the phone, she glanced at the screen. The time on the clock didn't tell her how long she'd been unconscious—hours or minutes. The screen was flashing *"18 messages from Randall Parleo."*

Anna cried bitterly. Crying was not even the right word. She was weeping. Not understanding anything, feeling only the aching pain in her heart, she roared and screamed on the floor and did not want to stop. The pain was so unbearable that she gasped for air, shouting and begging the heavens to give her answers.

Randall kept calling, and she finally found the strength to open the messages and read them.

He kept asking where she was, begged her to pick up the phone, and in one long message, he explained everything she wanted to know.

"Anna, please pick up the phone. I'm worried about you. Yeah, it happened once, right after I got back to Garth. We had a welcome party, and one girl kept harassing me. We danced for a long time and then we had some fun, that's it. I don't understand your reaction. Aren't we friends? Why are you suddenly offline and not answering me? I'm endlessly worried. Please answer me!!"

Anna read the message. It would seem that a thousand times. She suddenly burst out laughing hysterically. The situation was ridiculous, and she felt like a teenage girl with a broken heart.

Randall was still online, and she wrote:

"We're friends? We. Are. FRIENDS? "

"???" followed by a response from Randall.

"Do you sleep with all your friends, Randall? Are we friends?"

"Anna, I was sure that we understand each other. I never meant to hurt you. I thought we were on the same wavelength and having a great time!"

"Liar! I hate you!"

"Anna! Don't write to me insults. I'm telling the truth. That is why I calmly replied that I had sex. I didn't think it would hurt you. You must be having attention, too. That's okay with me. We're friends, and we didn't promise each other anything. Or do I misunderstand?"

Anna threw the phone on the bed. She couldn't stop crying. Resentment seemed to cut her heart. Randall had a point, but that didn't make it any easier. She was hurt. She couldn't hide it, couldn't ignore it, couldn't accept it.

She wanted to erase all their relationship from her life. Destroy all the photos, forget his name, obliterate everything they've been through together. She wished to never fly to Italy to see him. Now she hated this country, all the places, all the sights, all the people.

All of this, she wanted to erase from memory or…

Rewrite?

Or… rewrite…

Or—rewrite.

She grabbed the phone and ran outside.

Chapter 36

It poured. It seemed to have conspired with the girl and cried instead of her. Anna's tears dried up as if passing the baton to nature. For an hour, she was sitting in a nearby cafe, flipping through the Internet in search of tickets.

Tickets to Italy.

"I'll rewrite everything," she kept on saying, opening and closing bookmarks with tourist offers. The cost of tickets soared up, but Anna did not care. She was looking for so long, not because the astronomical prices of the trip worried her. She was waiting for some sign, some unknown signal that she should choose this date or this hotel, or this…

"Host Association Milan Tours."

"No way…" She pulled away when tours of the so-known platform flashed before her eyes.

"Host Association Milan Tours."

"Of course!" Anna made some kind of inhuman laugh and read aloud the opened banner.

"Host Association Milan tours" will help You choose the ideal accommodation with the best owners on the best terms. Need a quiet neighborhood? No problem! Cheaper housing? Easy Peasy! Are you traveling with a big company? Even better! Our super hosts are always happy to accommodate You and all your friends in their beautiful apartments for a fair price! No scam! No hidden fees! Only clean transactions beneficial to both tourists and hosts. Hurry! Students get a 30% discount!"

The plan lined up in a second. She'd fix it. She would make the journey perfect.

She would cut Randall out of her life and pretend nothing had happened. In place of this empty holiday romance would be a perfect, untainted journey.

Weird? Illogical? Let everyone who thinks that go smell tomato bushes.

"My life—my rules," Anna muttered and smiled. "A book I'm writing to myself. That's what my life is. I'm free to write whatever I want and tear out all the sheets that ruin the story. A new page, a new chapter. And from now on, I'll be the author, not everyone else."

With these heroic conclusions, the listeners of which were a coffee and a laptop, Anna began to leaf through the owners' lists offering their homes for rent.

"Michaelo Razzi. Pucci Str, 35… blah, blah, blah, clean, cozy mansion, blah, blah, your entrance… aha I see…" murmured the girl, scrolling down the suggestions and adding to favorites. "Dear reader, this is Milena Mirizzi, blah, blah… Wow! By the sea! Oh, wow, how much money do you want, Milena, my darling! Blah blah…"

She faltered.

"Randall Parleo. Fizzi Strada. A charming home for lovers of Baroque style and anyone who wants to spend unforgettable days and nights in the heart of Milan."

"Liar!" Anna yelled and spat on the monitor.

"Yacks!" commented the shocked Chinese man sitting nearby and witnessing the savory spitting.

"Excuse me, sir," Anna blushed and began to wipe the screen with her sleeve.

"Even more awful! Very more very more awful!" the Chinese made a grimace, trying to express his contempt. "Bendan!"

{Bendan from 'silly,' author's remark}

"Thank you!" Anna responded, not understanding at all, and grinned.

"Shi. Shi!" the Chinese replied and turned away in disgust.

{Shi from 'yes,' author's remark }

Anna closed the promo and went on reading. Several apartments she marked as *"Favorites,"* but then she saw this:

"Teo Reez. Apt 15-46 is the best offer you've ever seen—Luxury Villa near Santa Maria Delle Grazie for a mere penny. I don't want your money. I need your great impressions of my hometown. Yes. Such things happen!"

"Oh, no way! This is the Teo that Bernardo and Randall were talking about. Their hated rival that steals all their customers!"

She knew she would act out of resentment. She felt some dark, burning anger inside, which wanted to get out, wanted justice only in its perverted way—to make the offender as hurt.

Anna wanted Randall to suffer, to be hurt. She wanted him to lose her, to understand that he loved her, that it was not just a holiday hookup or some kind of friendship with benefits or whatever else he thought it was. But it was now that she saw in a second how things would unfold. She saw where it would lead, who would be hurt.

It was clear as day, and she wanted it. And she was about to do all required for it.

By clicking *"Contact the Host,"* Anna began to write a request to rent the villa.

Chapter 37

Teo answered briskly. He said he'd be happy to see her next week, and the villa would be free to drop by. They added to each other in social networks, and he briefly talked about the "Association"—almost everything Anna already knew from Bernardo and Randall.

As soon as he was on the friends' list, Anna viewed Teo's photos to see how the host looked like.

Teo was short for Mateo Reez, and he was born and raised in Italy, Milano. He was a tall, thin, charismatic young man three years older than Anna, dark-haired, with brown eyes. Not a super handsome man for everyone's universal taste, but he was not ugly either. He didn't smile in any of the photos. There was a sure "bad guy" flow with its stereotypical outfits—leather jackets, a cigarette in his teeth, a daring look, and carelessly styled hair. Almost all the photos were from some filming, concerts, and studios. Teo was very popular in Italy as a DJ and a musician. Everywhere were references to his albums, contacts, and demo versions of songs.

Music was not primarily in Anna's taste—to club hits, she was indifferent, but even not being a fan, one could conclude that content was indeed dope, with catchy and memorable beats. Anna scrolled his page for a few more minutes and, closing her laptop, headed home. The rain never stopped.

Chapter 38

"*I'll call you?*" a message came from Teo a few days later when Anna, having taken a shower after work, was preparing to go to bed.

"*Sure!*" she answered briefly and dialed his number herself.

He picked up after a few rings and with a video. Seeing him live, Anna was even taken aback for a moment, as she expected only a voice call, but in her heart, she did not regret it. The photos and a video were like a day and night. Teo looked completely different from the pics—he was smiling widely, dressed in a simple black T-shirt and white pants. In his hands, he had a guitar and suddenly said:

"I want to play for you."

Two things put Anna in a stupor—a sudden desire of almost a stranger to play the guitar for her, and the second was just a mind-boggling low, raspy voice with the velvet notes in it. She had never heard such a voice, even among famous people and musicians she admired, and this one phrase sounded in her head so loud and so delightful that she did not even bother to answer and continued to stare at the phone screen.

Teo laughed.

"Emm. Ow-kay, yes, I know. It is weird. But I want to play for you, I need to rehearse this song, and you will be my listener and judge."

And without waiting for the girl's answer, he started playing *Iris of Sleeping with Sirens*.

His voice was so unique that Anna seemed to dissolve into the music. It was all so sweet, romantic, and effortless. She listened to a beautiful song performed by this talented villa host and thought of how, from this moment on, she would write a happy story of the journey, full of positive emotions, such as she experienced now.

Teo finished playing, and they both laughed.

"Welcome to Italy!" through laughter, he muttered. "I wanted to break the ice and set you on a happy journey."

"Thank you, you certainly did!" Anna replied with a laugh too. "You're just mind-blowing! Nobody ever played the guitar for me! Thanks!"

"Meh, thanks. It is, of course, my cover, but the song is awesome. I want to rehearse it perfectly before the concert in Sweden. Are you packed? Coming?"

"Of course, everything as agreed. I have a plane in a day, and I'll be at the airport on Saturday."

"I'll meet you."

"What? Oh, thank you very much, but I can manage."

"Nonsense. You must have a suitcase full of meaningless women's things for the year ahead. I'm driving."

"Thanks," answered Anna blushing and admitted, "About the suitcase, that's true. But! Only the most necessary things!"

"No doubt!" Teo replied, and they both laughed. "Only for me not to forget anything, I need your arrival details. I went video to have an idea about how you look and not to lose you in the crowd. I have to admit. You look… exquisite!"

"Thank you!" Anna thought that she didn't hear compliments, even clumsy ones, for a long time, and it was enjoyable indeed. "I'll send it all to you."

"Great! I'm very pleased to meet you, Anna. I have a luxurious villa. You'll be thrilled! You gonna have a great time!"

"I'm excited!"

"Perfect. Well, we'll be in touch. And yes, you're a great listener—you do not squeak with delight."

They laughed again and ended the video chat on that positive note.

Until the day of the flight, Anna tried unsuccessfully to force herself not to sing *Iris* in full voice.

Chapter 39

Anna had been staring at the phone for several minutes with tears in her eyes. Exhaling deeply, she brought the device closer to her lips and pressed *"Record Audio Message"*:

"Randall, I live every day crying. I just can't wrap my head around how you could just sleep with some random girl after everything we've been through. I mean, I loved you, I really did, and what's there to hide, you know I still do, and yet you just closed your eyes to that fact and pretended it meant nothing. How comfortable that is—she follows you like a shadow, devoted fan, admires you, you can give her no promises. You're just a hypocrite. I'll redo everything that happened to me in Italy, and I'll tell you how, Randall. I'm going there again, and even if I get in trouble, I don't care, because you don't need me. Oh, yes, I forgot to say, an interesting coincidence—you lost a rent again, my host will be Mateo! The Teo you love so much! Thank you for a wonderful journey and a broken heart."

Randall immediately clicked to listen to the voice message and began to dial the phone number of Anna aggressively as soon as he heard.

She didn't want to answer, having decided that everything that would happen to her in Italy would be on his conscience, and she had not planned to give him a chance to dissuade her from this absurdity.

If he did not need her, she was unworthy of love, unworthy of anything good, because everything she possessed was not enough to win the love of this handsome man.

With that thought, she closed her suitcase and headed for the airport. The phone remained on the bed, blinking and receiving messages from Randall.

Chapter 40

The flight went unnoticed, but the girl's anxiety grew as she approached Milan. Having received the luggage, she took tentative steps to the exit, hoping not to make a mistake and recognize Teo among the waiting crowd.

Anna's flight was already a few hours late. She was nervous that Teo would not wait for her for so long. It was an ugly situation if he did, even though the reason did not depend on her. It angered her that a person offered to help, and she made him wait so long.

Coming to the last exit gate occupied by the greeters, Anna began to look around, trying to find Teo. It was easy to spot him. He stood leaning against a pillar and was dressed so impeccably that she almost opened her mouth—dark jeans, a leather jacket with chains, perfectly styled gel hair, and to crown it all, sunglasses and a straw in his mouth made him look like a model for some men's magazine.

Anna waved to him, and he noticed her at once.

Hmm, I hope he's not such a "bad guy" as he seems, thought the girl and walked over to Teo, introducing herself.

Teo took off his sunglasses and hugged her politely.

"How was the flight, Anna?" he asked with a smile.

What a voice he has! Her thoughts distracted.

"Fine, thanks. Sorry for keeping you waiting," she replied.

Teo took her suitcase and pointed to the exit.

"All is fine. Very tired?"

"Slightest. I slept well on the plane. Ugh, it's hot outside!"

"Yes, crazily hot today," Teo commented. "Here's my car."

In the parking lot, a couple of meters from them, Anna spotted a dusty Mercedes. A young man was sitting in the back seat.

"I have my best friend with me. I hope you don't mind?" Teo asked.

"It's okay," Anna smiled.

Teo opened the door for her. Inside the car, it was unbearably stuffy. The seat was so dusty that Anna snorted and half-jokingly pouted, refusing to sit in such dirt.

From inside the car came a chuckle.

"Your future wife is a real neat, Teo!" the lad laughed and held out his hand to Anna. "I'm Ricardo, call me Ri. Welcome to Italy!"

Anna laughed.

Ricardo seemed a witty and lovely guy. He was also dressed up to kill and kept his shades on, even in a car.

"Nice to meet you, Ri. I'm Anna." And turning to Teo, who was wiping the seat for her with displeasure, she asked if he was cleaning the seat thoroughly.

"As thorough as it can only be. Everything is clean. Glittering, as your eyes." Teo grinned and threw the cloth into the salon. "Sit down, Mademoiselle!"

"Merci." Anna finally settled in, still skeptical about the cleanliness of the car. "How far is it to go?"

"Not far. My villa is in the heart of Milan," Teo answered proudly and started the engine.

All the way, Anna studied him. He was not talkative, but friendly, very calm, and reserved. His appearance coincided with her ideas and expectations, but his voice, the manner of holding were unreal. He politely answered the girl's questions about the weather, music, or briefly discussed something in Italian with Ricardo, and every time he opened his mouth, Anna was in love with this voice. Deep, little husky, with a pleasant accent, he spoke every word clearly and smiled modestly. He had a piercing but friendly look in his eyes as if keeping some secret.

But the most striking detail, which was a real revelation to Anna, was his driving manner. He was like one organism with this iron body. He moved confidently, quickly, easily outrunning cars and going around the bumps, driving something resembling the levels in a racing computer game—so easily he could steer.

Teo could do it with his eyes closed. He was distracted, without losing concentration, humming the tunes, playing some castanets, gesticulating with both hands on a chastise his friend in Italian, looking at Anna.

And for the first time in life, Anna felt that she could relax in the car and not be afraid that she'd get into an accident or something would happen. This fear did not have any roots in the past, but Anna always wanted to keep control of her life, and to sit in the next seat to the driver meant trusting him with her life, not being able to control the developing events.

But now, it was so different. She felt that she could trust Teo completely, that he would bring her home, that everything would be all right.

She closed her eyes and dozed off.

But she dreamed the same thing that had haunted her for years...

Chapter 41

They were passing familiar places, and each time memories cut Anna's heart. She just recently strolled all these streets hand in hand with Randall. Here was a cafe where they had a snack, and here was the promenade, and here was the church, and here was…

"Anna?"

The girl turned around.

"Huh? What?" she asked, blinking.

"I asked if you'd been to Milan before," Teo smiled. "You have a nostalgic look."

"Oh, um… yes, very long time ago!" blurted out the girl. "But I didn't have time to see anything, so I came back to…"

"Fix it?" Teo finished.

Anna glanced at him, but her eyes suddenly filled with tears, and she abruptly turned the face away before Teo saw her despair.

"To… fix it," she squeezed out a confirmation, trying to keep the words as casual as possible.

"Perfect," said Teo, putting his hand on her shoulder and adding, "and you will make it."

Anna looked into his eyes. For a moment, it seemed to her that he knew everything, that he understood her without words, that he seemed to read all the expressions without having to explain anything.

She smiled meekly and looked out the window. Teo was turning into an enormous villa, surrounded by neatly trimmed trees. Security opened the gate, and Anna realized without a hint that Teo was not a poor man if such a high-class apartment belonged to him. She shivered and grinned:

"What did you say your job was?"

Teo looked at her slyly and spoke in a conspiratorial tone:

"Don't tell anyone. It's something trade-related."

Anna and Ricardo, who had heard the top-secret, laughed out loud. They lazily fell out of the car, and Anna looked around.

The yard was immaculate. A high carved fence enclosed the two-story villa with several terraces and a balcony. They decorated each corner with flowerbeds with small neat flowers of different colors.

Anna recognized only forget-me-nots and daisies, but all the flowers' splendor was beyond her knowledge, which she immediately regretted. She wanted to know the name of each flower. Amazed, she was gently touching them, inhaling aromas new to her and so unusual. The dog barked.

"It's been a long time, Signor Reez," said the guard, who approached Teo, shaking his hand.

"Lost at the studio. What's up? How did the tourists behave? Crazily, I imagine?" Teo asked politely.

"Nah, they're great lads. Good afternoon, Signora."

"Good afternoon," Anna replied to the greeting.

The man turned to Ricardo. "Good to see you, vecchio."

Ricardo shook his hand, and they continued the conversation in Italian. Teo took Anna's hand to lead her into the house.

They entered the grand hall, and Teo invited Anna to sit down on the couch while he would take the bags to her room.

Waiting for him, Anna looked around. Everything was clearly decorated with a pro hand of a designer. Various works of art hung on the walls. Elegant designer accents were everywhere—vases, statues, flowers. In the center of the room stood a glass table with an ashtray. A wide sofa was set up for relaxing and watching a huge plasma TV. There was another table in another corner, but a wooden and smaller one, with numerous discs, cassette headphones, and some musical odds and ends on it.

Teo left the room and asked:

"What do you think?"

Anna beamed.

"It's amazing. Your house is gorgeous. Thank you for accommodating me."

He hugged her slightly.

"Shall I show you the rest of the rooms?"

"Of course!" the girl exclaimed.

They went into the dark room Teo had set up for Anna. Its bathroom and dressing room made it an ideal option for a lady.

"You can raise the blinds," Teo explained. "But this room is always so dark because it's on the north side. However, I'm sure you'll like it. It's the best room in the house. Go upstairs."

They went up the stairs, and on the second floor, Anna saw several more luxurious bedrooms and a shared bathroom.

"Now, what do you think?" Teo asked again.

"That room below is the best one," said Anna, smiling.

"Nice. Then make yourself at home. I'm ready to leave in a few minutes. I'll just grab a guitar and a couple of clothes."

"Teo. Don't leave, please. You live here?"

Teo looked at her.

"Em… I've got another house. My mother, sister, and brother live there now. I'll go there."

"Stay, can you? You and Ricardo. Such a huge house, with so many bedrooms. I know little about the city. I'm not having the best time of my life, and I'd like some company. Is this possible? Are you very busy?"

Teo looked into her eyes as if trying to read the meaning of her words and finally spoke:

"I'm going down to tell Ricardo. I think it's a great idea to spend a week with a princess like you."

"Thank you," Anna smiled.

In a few minutes, having heard voices on the first floor, Anna herself went down. Ricardo and Teo were standing by the stairs, talking animatedly in Italian.

"What's the verdict?" she asked, looking at Ricardo.

He smiled widely and held out his arms for a hug.

"Of course, *Si!* The idea is just fantastic. What could be better than a sudden vacation with your best friend and his future wife?"

They burst out laughing.

"Thanks, Ri," hugging the guy, told Anna.

She hadn't even noticed that she had been hugging him for several minutes, staring intently at Teo, who was holding her other hand. Both guys seemed to feel her pain and understand her every action. And they wholeheartedly wanted to be there. But most likely, all this was only in her head, and she seemed to behave strangely to them.

Chapter 42

Anna entered the room and flopped onto the bed. She thought of only one thing.

Where was Randall? How was he?

Determined to call him and tell him she was in Italy, she opened her bag and was horrified to find that she had left the phone at home!

"Brilliant!" She threw the bag aside.

She wanted to hear his voice, to know his reaction. She kept replaying their last dialogue in her head, his calm confession that he slept with someone, and it was hurting her over and over.

There was a knock on the door.

"Yeah?" Anna asked mechanically, staying in bed.

Teo peeped in.

"How are you? Are you okay? It's quite late."

Anna turned and looked at him. For a moment, she was studying his features and then replied:

"All good."

Teo hesitated.

"Mmm… Okay, good night then."

"Stay."

"Huh?"

"Stay with me."

"I don't think that's a good ide…"

"Please." Anna stood up and approached him. "I'm your future wife, am I not?"

He smiled and flashed his eyes.

"You need to rest, Anna. Say nothing you'll regret."

"Stay."

She kissed him on the cheek. He kissed her on the cheek as well, without the slightest confusion, even not expecting her action. He hugged her tightly and laid near on the bed.

Teo was strong. Self-confidence was felt in his every movement, embrace, talk. And although his appearance did not fight on the spot, all the other advantages compensated for the slightest doubt. Anne felt nothing towards him except sympathy, a sincere admiration for talent and respect. His charisma was captivating. But it didn't shoot in the heart hard enough to make room for anyone else but Randall.

Teo halted, glanced slyly at the girl, and said, "Goodnight, Anna." And, straightening his blanket more comfortably, he turned to the wall.

"The rest is only after the wedding," he added with a grin and chuckled.

Anna threw a pillow at him and laughed. Next to him, she closed her eyes and fell asleep.

Chapter 43

"Anna! Anna!" Teo's voice broke into the girl's dream.

She opened her eyes anxiously.

"You were screaming in your sleep," Teo explained. "I'm concerned. What is wrong, a bad dream??"

The pillow was as wet with sweat as Anna herself. She was panting but could not remember a single detail of the dream. She could have guessed what it was about, but her head refused to cooperate. She felt ashamed and mumbled, lost in explanation:

"Sorry, Teo… Just a dream, nothing more. Perhaps, too many emotions from the travel…"

"You okay now?" he interrupted, handing over a glass of water.

Anna guzzled the contents and nodded satisfactorily. She wondered:

"Why are you dressed? What time is it?"

"About nine o'clock. I would wake you up anyway to invite you to have breakfast in an amazing tavern I know, but then I heard a scream."

"Forgive me."

"Nonsense. Are you sure you okay?"

"Yes, yes, of course. Nine o'clock… You're an early riser. I do not like to get up early, but breakfast at the tavern sounds good."

Teo smiled.

"I'll give you time to get dressed. You look awful!"

"Thank you!" Anna laughed.

Teo went out and left Anna alone with her thoughts. She tried in vain to remember the details of the dream. The scraps that popped up did not bring any understanding and, deciding that it was a waste of precious time. She got up and wandered into the bathroom.

She looked at herself in the mirror and grimaced. She looked awful, but the most terrible were fleeting thoughts—judgments about her, told by different voices.

"Beauty!" she heard Randall's voice, who did not tire of telling her this no matter what. *"Brainless ugly duck!"* was her stepfather's voice, more powerful, more deeply seated, as if saying the only possible truth for her.

She thought about everything. About Teo, her sincere desire to hurt Randall. She missed him. So much so that when she imagined his face, tears came to her eyes. She wanted to continue their affair. She longed for mutual feelings.

Why couldn't she be the girlfriend of such a handsome guy? Such a confident, charming, sweet, smart guy? Why was everything she always wanted unanswered? She's only worthy of being with a hairy, disgusting monster, like her stepfather type?

To repeat the fate of their parents—that's the path of the children? Was this fate not pleased with Anna's strong relationship with Mark? She was so sure she would marry him. Why such deep feelings were strangled by resentment, and now new deep feelings, when she was about to believe in having gained the second chance on love, are to be killed by anger?

Maybe this is not worth it, and cheating can be forgiven? Can we just not see it as a betrayal and start from the beginning?

Nonsense, he didn't need her. Randall didn't ask for forgiveness. He saw nothing wrong with the act. He just explained that he was a free man and could do anything. There was nothing to forgive, nowhere to go back. She swallowed her tears and muttered to her reflection in the mirror, "I still love you, Randall."

She sighed heavily and began to paint the self-confidence and happiness on her face. And this effect only makeup tools can achieve.

Chapter 44

Anna went out on the porch and, exhaling, walked to the car. Having seen the girl, Teo beamed and invited her inside. Ricardo stood beside the car, slowly smoking a cigarette. Anna smiled and hugged him.

"How are you, beautiful?" the lad muttered as he responded to the embrace. "Slept well... with Teo?"

Oh, I can't stand being addressed like that now, she thought.

Anna pinched his nose.

"Ay, nothing happened... with Teo!" she answered boldly and laughed. "But I slept well."

"Well, of course!" Ricardo winked.

"Listen, Ricardo..." Anna began.

"Ri," he corrected.

"Ri. I left my phone at home, and I wanted to ask for yours. I need to reach a friend of mine. Is this possible?"

"Of course! No problem." Ricardo handed her the phone. "Will you call? You want me to show you how?"

"No, no. I'll text him on social media."

"Oh, I see. Here's the browser; here's the app. Enjoy yourself."

"Thank you, Ricard... Ri!"

They climbed into the car and, turning on the volume of their favorite local tracks, and Teo and Ricardo started singing out loud. With trepidation, Anna logged into her account of social network and began scrolling through the messages. She was only looking for one person who sent... forty-five messages...

Forty-five messages, Randall! What is this nonsense? she thought and swallowed.

Eighty percent of the messages were generous, described in detail where-she-should-go-to-messages. A lot of exclamations and anger, threats to kill her if she continued to ignore the messages.

… And Randall was online.

Her hands trembled. She wrote a *"Hello"* and fell silent.

"Hello? Are you kidding me, Anna???"

The beginning was not very promising. Anna felt a sudden urge to send this person as far as possible, but something inside of her was even glad to see such a reaction. He did care.

"Hello, Randall," she added and smiled sarcastically, sending the message.

"I went crazily worried here! Where are you!"

"I wrote about where I was."

"What are you doing in Italy! You didn't mean it when you said you would sleep around. You said that out of anger, right?"

"What do you want, Randall? Leave me alone. I don't want us to talk anymore."

"Anna, this is a kindergarten. You're infantile and illogical. Where are you now? Please tell me."

"You wouldn't believe it."

"WHERE. ARE. YOU!"

"I'm at the residence of Teo Reez! What a coincidence. Small world."

"????????"

"I gotta go, Randall." And she signed out of the account.

Teo watched her. Feeling his eyes on her, she asked if everything was okay.

"Yeah, it's all right. You're magnificent. I look at you, and I feel like I can fall in love with you."

"Nonsense, Teo," Anna tried to joke, but she didn't like his tone. He looked serious.

"Watch the road, lover boy!" Ricardo snapped, helping to change the awkward situation.

"Well. Here we are," said Teo, reaching the delightful cafe with a summer terrace, with people walking to and fro. "Now, you'll be fed and distracted from all that busy mind of yours. I promise."

He kissed her hand, and they went to the place.

Chapter 45

"What a charming place!" Anna was genuinely delighted when they occupied the table.

"My favorite," Teo nodded, smiling. "I used to come here as a child."

Inside it was noisy but fun. Emotionally, as real Italians, people discussed news in the world and politics, everyday problems, and joys. Ricardo and Teo were actively involved in casual conversations, gesturing, and proving their point of view. Anna watched all this action with warmth and calmness.

"And now we invite Mateo Reez to the stage!" yelled a sweaty man with a microphone in his hands. The crowd roared in delight.

"What? Noooo!" Teo protested as soon as he heard his name.

"Te-o! Te-o! Te-o!" all cafe shouted in unison, applauding.

Wow, Teo is known in this place, as well as outside of it, Anna thought in surprise.

"Teo! Get on the stage, you lazy performer!" some signor encouraged.

Everyone laughed, and Teo, flattered by the attention, reached a well-worn scene in two jumps, grabbing the guitar on the move, which the waitress handed to him.

"What would you like to hear today, ladies and gentlemen?" he smiled, responding to a welcome of clapping hands and whistling.

"Whatever, just play already!" shouted one company. "Cose della vita!" the others were screaming louder.

"Sing to your girlfriend!" Ricardo shouted, causing Anna to blush for a second and kick him under the table.

"Yes, sing to her!" the crowd echoed. "Come on, Cose della vita!"

{Eros Ramazzotti—Cose della vita—author's note}

"Your wish is my command!" Teo nodded and masterfully commenced the famous Italian song.

All cafe customers were ecstatic. Anna didn't know the song, but from the first seconds, Teo's voice, as before, fascinated her. He looked her straight in the eye, making her blush even more and smile in embarrassment, as the crowd, believing they were a couple, whistled and encouraged him to change words by saying Anna's name.

No matter how wrong and awkward it looked, inside, Anna was pleased about such attention. He sang only for her. She saw it, felt it. He made it clear to everyone present, and he was proud of it. She's never been the center of anyone's world, even for several minutes.

She smiled broadly, and in her eyes, Teo read sincere gratitude. He smiled back and played the last chord, joking that he was actually singing the song for Ricardo. The crowd roared with laughter and, as he descended from the stage, thanked him and patted him on the shoulder as he made his way to the table where Anna and Ri were sitting.

Chapter 46

Anna threw herself on his neck.

"You're so talented, Teo!" she murmured admiringly.

"Thanks for the song!" Ricardo grunted, beaming. "You're so cute, but I'm engaged."

Teo has depicted the heartbreak and dramatically flopped down on the chair.

"Is this a joke?" Anna asked when they were all seated, and Teo went for a smoke break with two magnificent young ladies, who tirelessly praised his performance.

"What? Nooo. It's the truth. I'm getting married in September!"

"Wow, Ricardo!"

"Ri."

"Ri! It's just wonderful! Why didn't you tell me before? Felicitaciones!"

"I did not have a chance. My fiancee's name is Leticia, and maybe she'll join us some time, but she's staying with her aunt for the time being. You would have liked her."

"No doubt!" Anna confirmed. "She has great taste!"

Ricardo blushed and put his arm around Anna.

"I see Teo does, too," he whispered in her ear.

"Teo? Oh, no, between him and me noth…"

"Time. Everything takes time. Give him a chance, Anna. Teo is a great guy, caring and loyal. All that pomp is part of his image, people like that. It's like a mask, you know?"

"Ri, I understand, but…"

"Like your mask is. Behind it hides a girl who believes in love. You and Teo both believe in love deep down, but you chose not to show it. I see that. It all shows. You must both decide to be happy together or not. You are both worthy of happiness."

"Ricardo, I don't know what to say. I'm so grateful for your kind words. You're just amazing!"

"When I step away for a moment, all the 'just amazings' take my fate away!" Teo's voice came from behind them.

"Worth a try," said Ricardo. "I'm gonna go look for Marie, and you both have some chat meanwhile."

"A waitress now?" sarcastically wondered Teo, sitting in place of Ricardo and intending to clear his plate.

"Teo, thank you for the song. I imagined that you were singing only for me! It was great!"

"I sang it only for you, Anna."

"Thank you!"

"Welcome."

She looked into his eyes and tried in vain to understand what he was thinking. Teo smiled.

"The food's cold, Anna. Have something to eat. Don't overthink."

She breathed out, smiling timidly back, and set to a delicious meal.

Chapter 47

The next few days passed without the slightest remark on romance. Teo was as reserved as ever. Despite Anna's pleas, he took the weekend off from work and devoted time to sightseeing with the girl. Ricardo left to meet Leticia, and the meeting dragged on for a couple of days. All this time, Anna and Teo rode or wandered around Milan.

It was a completely different journey from what she had with Randall. There was no sunny mood and sparkling jokes, fooling around with friends, and freedom in everything. Teo made a very different impression on her. Although he and Randall were the same age, Teo behaved like an accomplished man. It was in everything—in his manner of speaking, of holding on, of acting. There was a weight of responsibility on him that made him grow up so early, and Anna wanted to find out what it was.

"Teo," she began as they sat in the hall. Teo was going through the guitar chords, writing a new track, and she was sitting next to him for what she imagined was moral support. She was distracting him constantly, but she despised the idea of going to sleep. "Tell me, does this mansion belong to you?"

"It was my father's," he responded, holding a pencil in his mouth and humming a tune.

"Does your father live here with you? Where is he now?"

"He died." Teo removed his pencil and looked at Anna. She blushed.

"Sorry, I..."

"No problem. It was a long time ago. My father was everything to me, and his death was a real blow to our family. My mother was left alone with us—three children—and she struggled a lot. As the eldest son, I inherited all dad's bills, family responsibilities, and all the other joys of his road when I was thirteen. Since then, I have worked to provide our entire family with food, give my brother and sister a decent education, and give my mother peace. I'm helping as much as I can."

"God, I'm sorry, Teo, I'm really sorry I asked."

"It's okay. I still think I'm doing infinitely little. As for the villa, I don't want to sell it because of my father's memory. Plus, it's a beautiful place. I am somewhat attached to Milan because of family circumstances. But the idea of renting the villa to tourists gave me a bunch of new friends from around the world, new experiences, and emotions. Among those who come, there are many musicians and other artistic personalities. To invite them here and show the city to me is real happiness."

"And you have a favorite job. You're a musician."

"Exactly. Music and I are one, and the audience feels it because…"

The phone rang. Teo paused and answered the phone.

"Yeah, yeah…" he muttered into the phone, and the emotions on his face changed at a furious rate. "I'll tell her."

Suddenly he looked darkly at Anna. She startled. When he put the phone in his pants pocket, she asked:

"What's up?"

Teo was silent for a moment but answered:

"Ricardo called. He and Leticia will be here tomorrow."

"Great news, right? What then…"

"And he also said that he got a call from a friend that you obviously corresponded with on Ri's phone, and that friend was vulgar, demanding of you, and ruined the date with Leticia."

Anna's breath got caught in her chest.

"Did he say who he was? Who was it?"

Teo came close to Anna and looked into her eyes.

"He wanted me to tell you to get in touch with him. He shouted that it was a matter of life and death. I think you should call him, Anna. I'll dial his number, and you can talk."

In a moment, he handed her his phone with the outgoing call named *"Randall Parleo."*

Teo took the guitar and left the room.

Chapter 48

Anna dropped the call. Randall called back immediately. Through the welling tears, she answered:

"Hello."

"Anna! I can't believe it!" Randall shouted into the phone. "Why don't you read my DMs! I have been writing into the void for a few days!"

"I left my phone at home. I took one from my friend to talk to you…"

"From that brainless Ricardo. Anna, I just can't believe it! Surely in your mind, you could not come up with anything less sophisticated than making up with Teo, whom I hate!"

"What?"

"Teo told me you were together, Anna. You didn't take long to get rid of such a deep love for me, did you?"

"Randall, how dare you say that? I guess Teo just said that because he doesn't feel the need to explain anything to you, but since you're talking nonsense, I guess there's no smoke without fire!"

"Anna, listen to me and don't you dare to hang up, or I'll come and smash Teo's face. You do not understand what you're getting into. Now listen to me. And be quiet, please. Are you crying? Anna!"

Anna sobbed so much that Randall's voice was lost in the background.

"Anna, please stop crying. Anna! Listen to me! I'm in Milan. I'll come to his villa today and pick you up. You're not staying there, you understand me?"

"Randall!"

"You understand me? Pack your bags and be ready by half-past five. These adventures must end. You know little about where you're going or who you're with. Teo's not the one you're supposed to be around. I hate him not just because he's stealing my tourists, Anna! Stop crying; you're listening to me or not!? Anna!"

"Leave me alone, Randall, go to your chick!" Anna shouted through her sobs. "Who are you to treat me like an object? I'm not going anywhere with you!"

"Listen to me, silly!" Randall shouted, barely holding back his emotions. "Anna, darling, listen to me. Teo's a dangerous man! You need to stay away from him, and it's not about us, me, or the chicks. It's about your safety!"

Anna could not even say a word more. She wept and did not even struggle with tears.

Teo entered the room, took the phone from her in one decisive motion, and pressed *"End."*

"This conversation is over," he muttered angrily. "Come here."

It was difficult for him to pull Anna away from the back of the sofa, which she was grabbing sharply to give vent to tears. He put his arm around her shoulders, led her into the bathroom, and washed her face. She continued crying, and he patiently wiped fresh tears with a towel again and again.

"Leave me, Teo," she squeezed out.

"Never," he whispered.

"Hey, children! I'm home!" They heard the playful voice of Ricardo entering the house.

"Go to Ri," Anna came up with an excuse. "Teo, please, I need to be alone now."

Teo stood up.

"I'll give you a few minutes while I go say hello."

At the door, he stopped and turned to say:

"He's not worthy of you, Anna. Whatever he told you in conversation, he's not worthy of your tears."

"He said he was coming to pick me up at five-thirty, Teo," Anna paused.

Teo's face changed.

"What did you just say?"

"Randall's coming here..."

"You're wrong about that." Teo's eyes were full of anger. "I'll kill him on the way here."

"What? Teo, don't say such things!" suddenly, under the influence of what Randall said to her about Teo, Anna got frightened and ran to him, grabbing him by the hand.

"Please don't be silly, Teo! If he comes, I'll go out and send him on his merry little way. That's all. Please, Teo!"

Teo suddenly pulled his hands away from Anna and pushed her away.

"You'll learn to respect me, Anna. And that man won't be here. Mark my words."

"Teo!" Anna was crying again, and despair and fear gripped her entire being. "Teo. Please stop saying that, Teo!"

"Stay in the room, Anna." His voice was unrecognizable. "Ricardo and I will go for a ride, and you shall stay here waiting for us."

He left the room abruptly, slamming the door. Voices were heard, and both guys quickly went. Anna rushed after them but found Teo had locked the door. She stood in the middle of the hall, strained by dread, unaware of what was happening, and it terrified her. She felt she was missing something important, but her brain refused to think about anything at all.

She ran out onto the balcony and looked down. Teo and Ricardo's car was gone. There were guards at her front door and near the gate.

The gate was locked.

Indeed, she didn't seem to know what she was getting into.

Chapter 49(A)

After several minutes of futile efforts to find the exit, Anna finally gave up. She went to the balcony again and looked around. From the height of the balcony, there were grand views and the main road. She tried in vain to look out for Teo's car. It was nowhere close.

Sighing and wiping her tears again, she wandered inside the house. As she walked around the rooms, she saw that one room was locked with the key still in the keyhole. This room was always in use, but she has never been there before.

Inside, the room was more like a pantry. The chaos of things in boxes and plastic bags everywhere. Piles of CDs and—books, books, books. Looking closer, it surprised Anna to find that all the books were in English—classical literature, English textbooks, magazines, newspapers, and even comics.

She opened the old edition of "The Old Man and the Sea" and smiled—Mateo Reez signed the book. After checking a few more textbooks, she was surprised to find that all the books belonged to Teo. They were scribbled incessantly with all sorts of notes and comments. It seemed that Teo had read every book more than once. The comics were painted with notes, obviously, when he thought of some compositions. In another box, she found a pile of scribbled copybooks, where Teo spent hours doing exercises to improve English.

It was a pleasant discovery for her. When he spoke, his English was perfect. Without the slightest accent, he could pass for an American. She could see now how much work had been done. But most of all, they matched in their passion for the language. She immediately remembered the days and nights spent at notebooks, and it was at that moment she seemed to become one with Teo in that. He was in love with language, like her. It was amazing.

She was glad she had come into this room. It helped her to discover Teo from a new side. But what she couldn't comprehend was Randall's warning. Why was he so concerned that she was with Teo? Maybe he was blackmailing him because even in this situation, they were competitors. Even though Randall did not need Anna, but just out of pure selfishness, he acted this way?

The door slammed. Dropping the books, Anna ran down the stairs.

Teo and Ricardo spoke sharply in Italian.

"Teo!" Anna cried out. "What did you do, Teo??"

"Calm down. Your lover is safe and sound, Anna. He was not at home. He was nowhere to be found, actually."

Anna felt an extraordinary relief, but again she was overcome by fear. Ricardo walked up to her and said:

"Anna, I don't know what's going on between you and Randall, but I don't like it. You decide. It is your life."

"Ricardo, I..."

"I'm hungry. I'll make us dinner."

"And Leticia?"

"She's not coming. We had beef."

"Because of what?"

He pivoted and went into the kitchen.

Wasting no time, Anna ran into the room for Teo. He was lying on the bed with his legs crossed and browsed the Internet.

"Teo," began Anna. "Look at me, please."

He immediately turned off the screen and put the phone away. They were silent for a moment. Anna broke the clouds, but Teo was ahead of her.

"I would have killed him, Anna."

"Teo, please don't say that!" Her voice shook again.

He stood up on the bed and showed her to a chair. He struggled to maintain a calm expression.

"Teo..."

"Anna," he looked at her coldly. "I don't care what you had with Randall. But I care that you don't respect me."

"Teo, what is that! I do respect you."

"You want to hurt him through me."

"I…"

"Now, listen to what I'm about to say. He doesn't need you, Anna. He talked to Ricardo on the phone in such a way that he was ashamed of you. He screamed for you to be returned, that you would never sleep with me. As if you are some item. Ricardo got into a fight with his girlfriend after because the whole evening he was evil and could not tune in to the romance."

"Look, Teo, I wanted to say that…"

"But I like you, Anna."

She paused for a moment, then continued timidly:

"I'm sorry about everything. And I had no intention of making you feel anything towards me, Teo."

"You had," he corrected quietly.

"I don't think I have the strength for a new holiday fling."

"Fling?" Teo raised an eyebrow. "There is no holiday fling, Anna."

"I guess I like you, too. But I don't think my heart can. I'm… I'm perplexed about everything, Teo. I'm not ready for any relationship. I'm not thinking straight. I…"

"Anna," he moved her chair closer to him and took her hand, "there is a mess in your head. Such a mess that it is visible even to passers-by on the street. Your behavior is utterly devoid of logic, but I see all the motives and reasons behind your every move. I'll tell you one thing. I'm not him. Not them. I'm Teo. And I like you, Anna, no matter what you do. Look at me. Do you hear what I'm saying? Listen carefully. I like you, no matter what. That won't pass. That won't change. It'll only get stronger. You cannot influence it. But you can accept it and give me the green light. And then, Anna, you will be mine. And you will always be mine. I don't share. I'm not giving up. And if you still don't understand—and I can see in your eyes that you don't—you *will* be mine, eventually. Not against your will, Anna, but because you will understand that you are worthy of a normal relationship, worthy of being near someone who respects and loves you. And this is me."

With that, he kissed Anna lightly on the forehead and stood up, having decided to give her some space.

Chapter 50

Anna left the room only a few hours later. Ricardo sat in the hall and watched TV, throwing darts at the target to distract himself.

"Ri?"

He looked towards the girl. His features were not as severe as before, but the discontent was still on.

"Ri," Anna tried again. "Listen, Ri. I'm so sorry I ruined your date, and I would have fixed it if I knew how."

"It's okay, Anna," Ricardo said calmly. "Don't bother."

"I'd like to talk to Leticia and apologize."

"Anna. Come on. I'm saying it's okay."

"I wanted her to come. Now, this incident won't give me a chance to meet her?"

"Anna, really…"

The phone rang, and on Ricardo's face, Anna read that it was Leticia calling. A little confused, he replied. A female voice was heard, and Ricardo listened to her with a solemn face.

Anna found nothing more clever than to run into him and shout into the phone:

"Sorry, Leticia!!!! This is Annaaaaaaaaa! Please, come here!!!"

Taken aback, Ricardo fell to the floor, and Anna fell on top of him, screaming apologies.

A second later, there was a hearty laugh in the receiver.

Ricardo tried to break out of Anna's grip, who blocked his entire left side in an attempt to grab the phone. To understand what Leticia said was impossible, but she eventually shouted "Okaaaaay!" to make herself clear, and all laughed out loud.

Anna rolled helplessly from Ricardo to the floor and stretched out like a starfish. Ricardo was breathing heavily, but he was smiling. His anger vanished.

"Thank you," he muttered as if regretting his words instantly.

"I hope she comes," Anna exhaled and looked at Ri. "Tell me where Teo is."

Ricardo stood up and gave the girl a hand.

"He went to the beach. Go find him. Let the driver take you."

Anna hugged Ricardo and whispered in his ear, "Sorry again, Ri."

Then she grabbed the scarf and ran outside.

Chapter 51

The driver took Anna to Genoa and, at her request, immediately left. It was already pretty dark when Anna found Teo. He sat on the beach and watched the sea. Raging, that night it was relentless, and the waves swallowed the moon now and then, hiding its icy light. Ten meters away from him, she stopped.

She was looking at him, but Teo didn't see her. How can people's feelings arise and pass quickly? Can sympathy move in hatred and respect in fear? Where is the guarantee that the relationship would not fall apart for years in old age, and a fleeting romance would not grow into love for life?

She looked at him, trying to understand herself. What was she looking for? Did she kill in her heart that distant dream of family and loyalty she had cherished since her youth? Teo reminded her of it. About this very dream, that she could be loved forever, deeply, and he could gift her this dream revived. She stood breathing full breast, trembling under the light of this moon. If she wanted, she could be loved.

But did she love anyone?

She looked at Teo. She saw all his virtues, his intellect, strength, confidence, and capabilities. She didn't know much about him, but she believed nothing terrible. She believed only her eyes. He could make her happy. But...

She didn't love him.

What did she know about love? Is love born out of passion? Is there love at first sight, or to love, you need to learn more about it? Can she not know the difference between love and passion, love, and sympathy? Or maybe she didn't love at all?

She didn't love him.

"I don't love him *yet*," Anna muttered and walked toward Teo.

He noticed her and stood up. They stopped a meter apart.

"We have to try, Teo," Anna said, looking into his eyes. "If you believe it's meant to be, maybe I will, too. But I don't…"

"I love you," Teo said and kissed the girl passionately.

As his lips greedily kissed hers and his tongue searched for an answer. The unfinished phrase *"But I don't yet love you, Teo"* rang in Anna's head. Still, she kissed him back with whatever she felt towards him.

Chapter 52

Anna stood on the balcony, breathing in the fresh air. It was late, and to her left, the sea rustled. The beach was plunged into darkness, and the sand seemed to have forgotten its usual ochre shades, reflecting only the gloomy mood of the night. Occasional raindrops were falling, trying even under the cover of night to remain undetected.

Teo knocked lightly on the doorway so as not to frighten the girl by invading her thoughts. But she still shuddered slightly when she discovered his presence.

"Want to be alone?" he asked calmly.

Anna turned to him.

"No," she smiled, afraid to hurt him. "Of course not. Join me."

Teo walked to the balcony and lit a cigarette. No matter how much Anna peered into his mysterious face, she could not read the emotions he was portraying even in the light of the full moon. Was he happy? Glad? Upset? Disappointed? It reflected none of these traits in his calm expression.

"I see you've settled the situation with our engaged couple," he said with a smile.

"Oh, I hope I have! I was ashamed that Rand..." she stammered, fearing the reaction of Teo to the name, but the lad's face, though he realized what she was about to say, has not changed.

"I'm glad everyone's okay," he commented. "And tomorrow we have grand plans, and Leticia will join the adventure."

"What plans?"

"It is a surprise!"

"I do not like surprises!" pouted Anna. "Come on, tell me now!"

Teo hurried to finish his smoke break to avoid explanations.

"Time for bed!" he joked paternally. "Bedtime!"

"Bed?" Anna raised an eyebrow. "You're crazy! What bed! We're going to the beach!"

"We are what?"

"Driving to the beach!" Anna grabbed him by the arm and began to drag force from the balcony outside because the idea did not inspire him much.

However, after some effort and impressive kicks, she pushed Teo into the street.

"I'm cold. Get in the car."

"Weakling!" she exclaimed jokingly.

"Weakling?! Look what you're wearing and look at me! Sweater vs. Vest? Get in the car, Mademoiselle!"

Comparing their outfits, Anna agreed that the night beach would look like an iceberg to him in this tight black T-shirt and black shorts. But the possibilities of her acrylic sweater he still exaggerated. She walked to the car, making unhappy faces.

"Won't you open the door for me to get in the car, sir?"

"Not this car." Teo smirked and smiled slyly. "That one."

He pointed to the half-light by the lantern BMW 740Li that stood in the yard's corner.

"What? Noooo." Anna didn't believe her eyes.

There was a signalization sound, and Teo rang the keys in front of her nose.

"A ride?"

"Aaaaaa! Of course!" the girl clapped her hands.

Teo beamed, clearly pleased with her obvious reaction to the luxury car.

They got into the auto, and a wave of questions rained down on him about how he had such a car when he bought it and why he hadn't given her a ride before. Teo only smiled at her banter, but was extremely pleased that such a small thing dispelled her bad mood, and he was happy to be a part of it.

The car belonged to his late father. After his death, he inherited it. He liked to drive a Mercedes more because it was a car he had earned himself, and he knew its price. BMW came in handy to dispel the clouds hanging over the villa due to recent events.

Teo drove her around the streets at night, and it was incredible. The same feeling of arrant confidence in how he drove made the girl completely relax and trust him. She looked around. Night Milan fascinated her.

All depressive thoughts dissipated in the air. She observed Teo—so peaceful and... smiling.

He smiled. Sight rare but meaningful much. He could not hide that he was glad of her presence. He was happy that she had agreed to give him a chance, and he was willing to do anything to keep her from changing her mind. But right now, he was just glad that he could bring her smile, and he smiled at it himself.

They stopped at some diner selling fast food through a window at night hours. While Teo was ordering the pizza, Anna stood by the car and tried to arrange her hair, ruffled by the wind, while riding around the city.

A couple of guys drinking beer on a bench nearby and, surely far from being shy, whistled in her direction comments and questions with the standard "Where do you dress up so neat, chick?", "Come with us, eh?" and so on.

Teo took the pizza and shouted back to the group, "She's mine, you losers!" He showed them the known sign from his fingers and quietly got into the car. Anna quickly jumped after him, fearing that the young people under the influence of alcohol would get angry, and there would be a fight. But those only sprinkled different "courtesy" in response, without a hint of a serious counter-attack.

Anna looked at Teo with displeasure, though inside, she felt a certain pride in the short sentence he had thrown at them.

"Pizza!" Teo licked his lips and held out the box to her. "It is vegetarian. Save a piece for me."

"I'll eat everything! And be fat!"

"Well, I've always liked the fat ones," he muttered.

"Oh, really? So I'm not your type now?"

"You are, to be honest, a little bony and silly. And you snore a lot at night. But generally, everything's fine."

"What?" Anna laughed. "I did not expect such a roast! I thought I was striking you with my beauty!"

"Never mind. You just have to eat more pizza. And then you'll strike me with your beauty. I will wait."

After receiving a couple of slaps, Teo started the car, and they turned towards the beach.

Chapter 53

The sea calmed down completely when they reached the beach. There was almost no wind, and the moon was shining at full strength, letting everyone know that she was the only queen of the night. Teo stopped the BMW right in front of the beach and seemed to be right in the center of the bright moonlight.

They just sat in silence for a few minutes. The night was so enchanting that the words seemed to ruin this magnificent idyll if pronounced, and the couple knew it.

After a while, Anna finally spoke:

"What an alluring, magnetic night, Teo, isn't it so?"

He looked at her and said:

"Like you."

Anna flushed and looked down.

"I wrote a song for you. And now is the right time to perform it." With these words, he climbed into the back seat to get a guitar.

"A song?! For me?" she glanced incredulously.

"For you." Teo smiled and ran his long, graceful fingers along the strings. "And now you'll hear it."

"Teo, I…"

But Anna did not have time to finish the sentence. A lyrical melody poured over her. Teo, as if knowing what effect his voice had on her, used it to the maximum. His chords were mesmerizing. Anna didn't know how to react, how to listen, how to breathe. It filled her with so many emotions. They were so different, fighting among themselves, that even the night could hardly hide the internal conflict from detection. But Anna tried to focus on Teo, how amazing he was, how talented, how… in love…

He seemed to be really in love with her. Every note, every chord showed his feelings with such force and pride that Anna was afraid to mess up this perfect picture somehow. But treacherous thoughts rushed into her head uninvited, tearing her heart apart.

She tried to hide the little tears running down her cheeks. She was thinking about Randall. It would seem that the longer Teo sang, the more her heart ached for Randall. How was that possible? How could she love Randall so much? Why didn't his action kill her feelings? Why now, sitting next to the perfect guy, she was thinking about Randall? Why were the lyrics associated only with him? Why was she looking at Teo and seeing Randall? What did Randall do that was so special to sink so deeply into the very depths of her soul?

Teo finished and smiled. An alarm immediately replaced his joy when he noticed that tears were flowing down Anna's cheeks.

"Anna? Are you okay?"

Suddenly Anna burst into hysterical laughter. Not to spoil everything, she jumped up abruptly, threw herself on Teo's neck, thanking him for the beautiful composition.

"This was unbelievable!" she exclaimed, not knowing why she was laughing.

Teo was confused, but he didn't resist the hug.

"Did you like the song?"

"Sure! And now—to swim!"

"What?"

Anna, still laughing, ran across the sand towards the sea.

"Anna!" Teo shouted after her, leaning out of the car. "Anna, what nonsense, what are you doing! Ice water, Anna! Come back now!"

Anna heard nothing. She laughed and ran to the water. Teo followed her with quick steps.

"Anna, stop it! Come on! Don't get into the water!"

As soon as she reached it, Anna threw herself into the water. Her body seemed to be pierced by thousands of needles, but her soul felt so good. She did not laugh anymore. She cried loudly. The sea swallowed all her sobs, and even she could not hear herself crying.

"Anna! You're so silly! What a kindergarten!" Teo walked into the water and, grabbing the girl in his arms, dragged her from the icy water.

Wrapping her arms around his neck, she kissed him and laughed again.

"You smell like fish!" he winced. "That is disgusting! Yack!"

"Really, what horror!" she laughed. "Look, I'm covered in scales!"

"What a clever deed!" Teo pinched his nose and kept moving back to the car. "Today, you sleep on the mat in the corridor! You should have thought of diving at a time like this!"

Anna laughed and stuck the sleeves of her pullover, soaked in the fishy smell, up to his nose.

"You will walk next to the car as a punishment for your frivolity," he grumbled as he opened her door. "Stop now! Take that shirt off before you sit down!"

"Miserable whiner!" the girl laughed, pulling off her sweater. "Is that better?"

"Much… better…" he commented, stopping to look at her naked body with no sign of underwear.

Anna threw the wet jacket in his face and ran into a joke fight. Barely disarming her in the backseat, Teo covered her entire body with kisses. He didn't go on, didn't hint at anything. He just enjoyed kissing her endlessly. Kiss her everywhere. Where he couldn't before. Where he always wanted.

She responded to his every touch, moaning, saying his name. His touch aroused her, and she wanted him. But every time she took the initiative, the brain seemed to stop her, and she was glad that Teo was not moving to the next step.

"Anna, you smell awful," calmly noticed Teo.

"Thanks," she smiled.

"I can't take it anymore, honey. It's horrible."

"It's all right, darling. I don't like you either."

After exchanging kicks, they moved to the front seats and drove home. The moon was the only witness to everything on the beach.

Chapter 54

The next morning Anna woke up in an excellent mood. Teo had been up for a long time. His early risings were impossible to get used to, but he always gave her time for a good night's sleep.

She lazily pulled on leggings and a top, made an elegant tail, leaving some strands of hair loose, washed her face, and went out into the hall.

Teo was sitting with some lads on a sofa, drinking beer. Just noticing the girl, he waved her to join the group. Anna obediently went in their direction.

"It's her," Teo muttered, and his friends whistled appreciatively. Anna made a questioning face.

"So that's who stole the heart of our impenetrable Teo!" exclaimed the lad, head to toe covered in tattoos.

"Beautiful," the second commented.

Anna grimaced at the comment. Teo hastened to shut the others, changing the subject to a discussion of the latest club tracks.

Anna sat down next to Teo. Her eyes fell on the phone on the table. She had to try again. She needed to know if Randall was okay. And she was worried about her job. She suspected to have lost her teaching position, and her ridiculous explanations and invented excuses for a sudden departure had exhausted all time limits.

And Mark… He worried about her endlessly, and she was selfish to leave like this, explaining nothing. And Mom… She was the one who indeed went crazy for not hearing from Anna!

The reality, with all its demands for rationality, overwhelmed her. She felt that she had acted frivolously and irresponsibly.

"Teo," she turned to him resolutely. "Can you give me a phone?"

Her voice faltered. She expected Teo's face to change, dismissing her request with threats of trouble if she brought it up again.

"Certainly," he replied and pointed to the phone on the table.

"Oh… Okay… Thanks." Without waiting for Teo to change his favor, she grabbed the device and hurried into the room.

Chapter 55

As soon as she closed the door behind her, she fell onto her bed, logging in social media and e-mails as she went, scanning messages and missed calls.

The first thing she did was call her mother and apologize a million times for her shameless behavior, assuring her that everything was fine and that she would be back in Mining City in a few days.

Then she found Mark's number, and without reading fifteen messages from him, she immediately dialed.

"Yes?" The familiar voice warmed her heart at once.

"Mark, it's me," she began. "I'm sorry I didn't explain, but I had to leave."

"Anna? God, finally! I can't believe it! Where are you?"

"I'm back in Milan."

"What are you doing there?"

"I think I'm getting into trouble, consciously."

"What are you talking about?"

"Mark, are you coming?" A woman's voice came from the background.

"Yeah, yeah, give me a minute," Mark said to the stranger.

A pang of jealousy shot through Anna. What was that? Hurt ego, maybe? She winced at the discomfort. She hadn't even considered the possibility someone would occupy that Mark's life... other than her. Typical female selfishness. Crab mentality. And the girl's voice reminded her defiantly that Anna was not a wedge of light. And it was painful to hear.

"Ahem. Are you busy?" Anna asked grimly.

"No, no. Anna, are you okay? Get outta there. I don't know what's going on in your head, but I advise you to stop and not make mistakes you will regret."

"Maaaark!" the female's voice called again, louder.

"It's all right, Mark. Thanks for caring. I'm just having a relationship problem," Anna wanted to know Mark's reaction to that statement. Was he as uncomfortable as she was?

"Um… what's the problem?" There was indeed a note of discontent in his voice.

"Randall slept with someone. And I flew to Milan to be with a guy he hates, to hurt him."

"What a… wise plan, Anna. Are you thirteen?"

"I know, it's silly… but it hurt so much that I couldn't think of anything else. But it doesn't make sense because Randall doesn't care about me."

"Well…Hmm…And this guy?"

"What guy?"

"The guy he hates doesn't care about you, either?"

"I don't know. Teo's a good man, and he admitted to having feelings for me."

"What feelings?"

"Mark, I don't know! What a question! He even confessed he loved me, but I guess he said that because the situation was good and just out of passion. We don't know each other very well, so…"

"I see. Anna, I have to go now. I'm late for the movie, sorry. I'll just tell you that the best thing to do when you see a storm coming is to put down your umbrella and not leave the house at all. Take care. Ciao."

"Thank you. Ciao, Mark."

He hung up. Anna stared at the blank screen for a moment, trying to control the discomfort of her conversation with Mark, but she calmed down and began to answer the messages. Letters were infinitely many, and all had to be answered. Still, flashing nine messages from Randall she studiously ignored, focused only on responding to all emails and letters from friends and family.

Chapter 56

When she was done, she turned off the phone and tossed it on the bed, ready to return to her guests. As soon as she got out of bed, she stopped and, vainly fighting curiosity and despair, grabbed the phone again and opened Randall's chat.

"Anna, please answer me. It can't go on like this. I need to talk to you."

"You have to stay away from Teo. He's not who you think he is."

"Anna, please write to me. I'm going insane with worry. You're precious. I have such a mess in my head right now."

"Anna, we need to see each other."

"How dare you, Anna!"

"Everything is ruined. I just have a brain drain. I can't do anything. I don't live. I don't eat, I don't go out. Anna, answer!"

"I need to see you and discuss something."

"Anna, please, beautiful, let's meet."

"Anna, I will never stop writing, only when my heart stops. But even then, I will appear to you in a dream until I drive you crazy."

She exhaled heavily and wrote back.

"I'll think of something."

The noise of the party filled the hall. She logged out, erasing all history, calls, and open correspondence, then went to the mirror and looked at her reflection. Her whole soul longed to see Randall. What if he wanted to tell her he loved her and regretted what had happened? She had to find out at all costs.

From the hall came the sound of guitar playing. Teo was singing a song, and there were many admiring female voices. She shared their groanings because the talent of Teo was undoubted. She went out into the hall and discovered him playing "I Will Follow You Into The Dark" {Death Cab for Cutie, author's note}, surrounded by a few chicks clearly in love. The ladies kept their eyes on him and seemed to struggle to sit as close as possible. There were so many people in the hall that Anna could not help staggering when she saw the crowd.

"He is smoking hot, isn't he?" Ri whispered in her ear.

Anna shook her head positively.

"Leticia came??"

Ricardo beamed.

"Where is she? Where? Introduce us!" Anna clapped her hands.

He led her through an almost impenetrable wall of flesh into the kitchen, where a charming, plump girl stood beaming. She was gorgeous. Her immaculate white dress accentuated her figure, her shoulder-length curly hair glistened brightly in the chandelier light, and a necklace of beads complimented her already elegant image.

Anna ran into her with a hug.

"At last! Oh!" she exclaimed. "My salvation has come from the company of these plain men!"

Leticia giggled and assured her that Anna's life was saved from that moment on. Teo finished the song in the hall and earned a standing ovation and applause. The girls groaned and asked for an encore. The crowd got back to loud talking again, ringing glasses with alcohol and discussing the trivial things.

Chapter 57

"Can you help me with the snacks?" Ricardo asked the girls, and they both nodded.

Anna and Leticia became friends in a minute. In peeling potatoes and other vegetables, they discussed their lives and dished about everyone around them.

Several other girls joined them. Anna was pleased to be finally in female society, and all went on swimmingly together.

Suddenly, the applause was heard from the hall, and people shouted in chorus, "An-na! An-na! An-na! An-na!"

"What the…" began Anna, but Ricardo smiled broadly and grabbed her arm, pulling her into the crowded room.

Anna was genuinely horrified. As she pushed through the smiling, unfamiliar crowd, she struggled to think of a rational explanation for the situation. Ricardo pushed her into the center of the room, where Teo was leaning on his guitar and smirking.

"Teo, what the…" The second attempt to discover the situation was…

Interrupted.

Because Teo took her in his arms and kissed her passionately.

At the same moment, the lights dimmed, Ed Sheeran's romantic song "Perfect" came on, and bubbles of different colors appeared in the air. There was a smell of coconut, and Anna saw one guy (already very, very drunk one), pulling light silk, which Anna had not even noticed before, from all the pieces of furniture, exposing huge bouquets of flowers—green roses and tons of cups with coconut cocktails.

They were her favorite flowers. How did Teo know? Anna's eyes widened in surprise. She looked at him admiringly, spinning slowly in the dance.

"Surprise," he whispered. "I know it's nothing compared to what I'd like to show, but take it as a sign of my admiration for you." And he sang along to the music.

Anna couldn't find the words. She just hugged him tight and closed her eyes. She could only hope that he would feel her gratitude. Everyone clapped. When the song ended, Teo stood in the center of the room and shouted so everyone could hear:

"It's her. And I love her."

Everyone whistled and whooped, grabbing the cocktails. There were shouts of approval and admiration. Many girls enviously pouted and said they were wasting precious time at this party.

Anna felt happy to be dressed up accordingly to the moment- her black dress complimented the bright makeup, and her wavy curls framed the face most exquisitely. She felt the looks of admiration and the genuine compliments on her beauty filled her—and Teo—with pride.

"You're so amazing!" Anna exclaimed." I'm shocked! These are my favorite flowers! How did you know??"

"I…" Teo began mysteriously when the phone rang, and his face changed as he looked at the screen.

It was Randall.

Immediately realizing who was calling, Anna grabbed Teo's hand, trying not to give him the chance to pick up.

"Teo, forget the call. Teo, look at me. Such a romantic moment, please, Teo, let's not spoil it."

Teo gently disengaged his hand and, as if looking sadly at Anna, went into the kitchen. Anna tried to run after him, but as luck would have it, many people started coming up to her with congratulations, endorsements of Teo's gesture, advice on how to keep love alive forever, as if they had announced a wedding.

Tarrying two minutes was enough for Anna to miss the phone talk. When she ran into the kitchen, Teo was standing by the fridge, drinking juice. There were a couple of other people in the kitchen, but they evaporated as if they felt the tension.

"Teo. Did you talk to him? What did he say? Why had he called?"

Teo's eyes flashed.

"Maybe you can explain why Randall called me when I decided to surprise you, Anna?"

"Teo, I… I don't know."

"Well, then, I will throw some light on such an important question. You agreed to meet him. And I was clearly not informed."

"What? I just said I'd think about what I could do, I…"

"Do I look like a fool, Anna?" roared Teo. "Don't you know the concept of respect? How long can you throw that filth in my face?"

"Teo, stop! Don't say that! I do respect you!"

"Then what kind of meeting is this behind my back? Randall called to inform me you wanted to see him at the center tomorrow, my love! Can I give you a ride to such an important meeting? What time did you agree? At six? Five o'clock? Maybe the meeting will be held at night?"

He tossed the juice box into the bin, turning it over. Anna started to gather up the scattered food, but Teo stopped her and held her in both hands, looking into her eyes.

"Teo, you're hurting me!" Anna cried, and he released her at once.

"Sorry, I didn't mean to."

"I didn't make an appointment with him. Let me talk to him!"

"Talk? Anything else?"

"I want to know what he's talking about! He asked me to meet him to clear things up, and I said I'd think of something."

"So, you want to see this man after what he did?"

"What?"

"He said you didn't want to talk to him anymore because he slept with some girl. And yet when he whistles at you, you run wheedling to him like a dog."

Grabbing a glass of water from the table, Anna poured it into Teo's face. For a few seconds, he stood as if thunderstruck, and Anna thought he would hit her. His eyes filled with fury, and Anna automatically covered her face with her hands, expecting a slap or a blow.

"It was the first and last time you did something like that."

Opening her face, she saw Teo step away from her. He was breathing hard and struggling to have a command of his brain.

"Begone," he said through clenched teeth.

"I'm not a dog," Anna replied bitterly as she headed out of the kitchen.

Chapter 58

Anna ran into the room and slammed the door violently. Having noticed the mood, Ricardo hurried after her to find out what was wrong.

He knocked timidly, but Anna threw a pillow at the door, warning whoever it was to get out.

He opened the door a little and asked what had happened. Seeing that it was Ri, Anna ran to him, took his hand, and sat him down on the bed.

"Teo heard from Randall that we would see each other."

"What?"

"Yes, I know, I know. But Ri, listen to me. It's not as simple as you think."

"Anna!" Ricardo's face betrayed shock. "Is that why you were arguing in the kitchen?"

"Yeah. Ri, listen to me. I need your help. Please get Teo to let me go see Randall only once."

"What?? Anna, are you out of your mind?"

"Only you can talk him into it. I don't have a phone. But I need to see Randall. Please, Ri, help me. You're not only Teo's friend, but you're also mine. Please, help me!"

"You should hear yourself now!" Ricardo replied angrily, shaking his head. "Why are you trying to ruin your budding relationship with Teo for this guy?"

"Ri, please. It's not that simple…"

"I'm not silly, and I know what your 'not that simple' is. You love Randall, Anna."

Tears welled up in Anna's eyes, and she could no longer hide her despair.

"We parted terribly. I can't move forward knowing that I didn't talk to Randall, didn't hear his point about some of the things that happened between us. I didn't give us a chance to say goodbye in a human way. Randall was kind to me, except…"

"He was having fun with you, and you were thinking about all kinds of love in your head. Listen to what I tell you. You really need to meet Parleo, not for a new drama, but to finally see him with different eyes and understand that he's not for you and that you, with your silly actions, may lose a decent guy who would do anything for you."

"Ri, please, please, help me!"

Ricardo sighed heavily.

"Promise me you won't break Teo's heart. He's like a brother to me, Anna. And I don't want to do anything to hurt him. You promise me you will deal with this once and for all and end whatever's going on between you and Randall."

"Thank you, thank you, Ri!" Anna hugged him tightly, and he left the room, leaving her to hope that she wouldn't have to go to Randall against Teo's will, jeopardizing everything they were trying to build.

"God, help me…" she whispered and closed her eyes.

Time was lost in the slumber that descended upon her.

Chapter 59

Anna woke up to a noise in her room. It was Teo, trying to change as quietly as possible, but he dropped the hanger, and it crashed to the stone floor, waking her up. She glanced at him sleepily and caught the guilty look on his face for having inadvertently awakened her. His usual sullenness quickly replaced it.

"Teo…" Anna whispered.

"Sorry." He hurried into the bathroom.

Teo was in the shower for about half an hour. All the while, Anna wondered if Ricardo had talked to him or not and if she should have brought it up again. Teo interrupted her thoughts himself as he entered the room, wet and smelling of lime.

"Go ahead. Meet him," he retorted, covering his face with a towel.

"What?" Anna couldn't believe her ears.

"I said, go ahead, meet Parleo if it makes you happy. You didn't have to send Ricardo to me for that."

"Teo, I just…"

"You would have gone no matter what."

"I wouldn't go if you didn't want me to, Teo."

"You are not a prisoner in this house, and I am not your master. Do whatever you please."

"Teo, I told you I wouldn't go if you didn't approve."

"Well, I disapprove, Anna. But don't be disingenuous. My opinion won't stop you. So that your conscience may not spoil your meeting, I say you may go to Randall, who is expecting you tomorrow morning."

"Teo, that's a frivolous accusation! I want to meet him, to dot the i's and cross the t's, and nothing more."

"I don't want to hear anything else, Anna. I am tired." Teo gasped and crawled under the covers. "It's four in the morning, and I have to get up early tomorrow."

"Teo!"

"Goodnight, Anna. I'll go to work tomorrow, and I'll even be happy to give you a lift to your lover, as I mentioned in the kitchen. Be ready by eight in the morning, darling."

"Stop that!" Anna cried, jumping on top of him and covering his mouth with a kiss.

Teo didn't expect this. At first, he resisted and tried to push her back onto her side of the bed, but she firmly grabbed his hands and put them on her buttocks. It instantly stopped resistance. Teo took the initiative, and the next second, they were kissing each other. Anna wouldn't let go of Teo for a second, but when she realized he was suddenly ready to move on that night, she pulled away from him.

"What? Noooo…" he moaned. "Don't be silly, Anna."

"I am not ready for *that*, Teo!"

"Anna, don't act like a child," Teo grunted.

"I am not ready!"

Teo stopped and looked into her eyes.

"Oh, really. I'm sorry to be blunt, but I am thinking you had guys before me. And your so familiar to me *partner* is making me vomit. So, do not be a hypocrite."

"So, I'm a hypocrite, and you're an angel?!" Anna sat up in bed and pulled away from Teo, glaring at him.

"I'm not an angel. Now get back to your original position and stop talking."

"You've ruined everything."

"Ruined everything? Anna, sometimes I think you talk no sense. I didn't ruin anything, and I want you."

"Some other time," she snapped, pulling her clothes back on as she got out of bed.

"Oh, brilliant!" shouted Teo. "Can't you just enjoy things? You know what! Forget it. Goodnight."

"Goodnight," Anna answered and left the room, slamming the door behind her.

Chapter 60

She went out into the hall and plopped down on the sofa, stepping over the bottles. Thoughts swarmed through her mind. Teo didn't see the logic in her reaction, but Anna saw the situation in a very different light.

It was the last night before she could meet Randall, and she had to make up her mind to move on with Teo. And she couldn't do that. Silly? Yes. Cruel? Yes. But to whom?

Why did she keep following that destructive plan when she knew that if she was with Teo, it would just make Randall feel uncomfortable, as he couldn't stand Teo. It wouldn't hurt him at all because he didn't love her. Teo would only be glad because, in his eyes, it is a proof that Anna was ready to be with him, that she had feelings for him.

It was cruel *to her*. She persisted, intending to punish herself. That she could not be ideal, whom Randall would fall in love with. That she could not love Teo, but he was worthy of reciprocal feelings. That she was ready to run like a dog when Randall whistled, and with all this, still hoping that his heart could change when he knew that Anna was with Teo.

She began to cry aloud. Some unknown force continued to drown her in the circumstances she had designed when that same pain stabbed her in the heart for the first time. Why couldn't she stop everything, as Mark had told her on the phone, pack up and go back to Mining Great City? What was she doing here?

Her shoulders, shaking with sobs, clasped in familiar hands. It was Teo.

"It's worth the Guinness book of world records for the weirdest reaction to a guy moving on to sex," he murmured, smiling in the darkness.

"Leave me alone, Teo," she barely squeezed the words.

"Never." He took her in his arms and carried her back into the room.

Putting her on the bed, he began to wipe her tears with light movements of his lips.

"I love you, silly. I was thinking now. I am sorry. Before you, I only had girls I picked up at concerts and parties and only for 'sleeping and forgetting in the morning.' I just desire you. I did not mean it to be offensive. I am sorry."

He grinned and went on softly, "But you are my love. Your body is a work of art for me. I adore you, every cell of your body, your laughter, your gestures. You are my ideal. I found you, and I don't want to lose you. Never."

With that, he began to cover her body with kisses and take off her clothes.

A private fear had haunted Anna. She had no other reason to prevent what was about to happen. She was not ready at all. But she did not want to hurt Teo.

She whispered inaudibly, "Sorry," and Teo proceeded.

Only the apology wasn't meant for him.

Chapter 61

"No, please, stop! I can't!" Anna screamed, pushing Teo away.

"Calm down! I stopped," he said and leaned back on the other side of the bed, burrowing into the covers, bewildered.

"Why were you so persistent! I was not ready!" Anna jumped up in horror, realizing what she has let happen.

"You sound like I did something against your will!"

"Teo!" shivering, Anna ran to the bathroom to take a hot shower.

She was numb. Ruthlessly scrubbing the body with a sponge, as if it was dirt, and showered Teo with curses. He did it on purpose! Why would he push her for more? Why! What was she thinking?

Teo walked into the bathroom, and she started punching him.

"What have you done, Teo! Did you do that on purpose?"

Grabbing her elbows, he said:

"Anna, stop yelling. I did nothing on purpose. Nevertheless, I'm not made of marble. All this time, I've endured you stopping me with all your signals when it came to sex. But look, before meeting Randall, you agreed to go for it so it would probably hurt him more? Well, now, he's going to be in a lot of pain, and I guess I did you a favor here. Oh, no, of course not; what am I saying! Of course, you are so in love with me that you desired me too. I will marry you, and we will always be together, I'm a great guy! Now, throw the dice, Anna!"

With that, Teo pushed Anna's hands away from him and walked out of the bathroom.

Anna slid down the wall, weeping bitterly.

Chapter 62

Teo returned a few minutes later and, throwing a wide bath towel over her, led her out of the bathroom into the bedroom.

"Anna, listen," he said quietly, wiping away her tears. "Stop crying. Nothing terrible happened. Nothing is so terrible to be so grieved. Calm down, please. And get it out of your head that I'm some kind of monster. I was just so enjoying the moment. But I had no idea you did not want me as I wanted you!"

"I was not ready!" she retorted through her tears. "You think I do not deserve some time?"

"No, I don't think so. But I think you are clearly overreacting."

"I did not want it!"

"Even though you are hurting me now really bad, I will say nothing to that. I love you, Anna. And you have no idea for how long I have loved you."

"What! Love me? You do not pressure the ones you love!" Anna threw a towel at him and began to dress up quickly.

Teo sighed.

"Let us go out to breathe some air. I feel like my head will explode now. I'll start the car," he said calmly, leaving the room.

"Randall warned me not to trust you!" Anna blurted out, immediately regretting what she'd said.

Teo turned and glared at her.

"Repeat that."

"You heard me…"

"You know, Anna. I swallow everything from you. What Randall told you doesn't surprise me. But seeing you trust this loser who used you just for fun just hurts me. I will tell you once again that—even if I were happy to have a relationship with you—I would never create one through force or against your will.

"However, as I understand, what you just said comes from your conversation with Randall, and I'll tell you what. No matter how bad he makes me look to you, none of this is true. Randall doesn't know what he means by trying to trick you into staying away from me. I have known him for many years, and as lads, we had an aversion to each other. But his hatred is not about competition for the tourists. It goes from the usual envy of my money and position. Randall and I took part in the same musical contest, which gave rise to huge career opportunities.

"He's a great musician if you don't know, but not great enough. Because I won the contest, and I wasn't even really fighting for the award at the time. I was living a sedentary life, dabbling in drugs, sleeping with all sorts of girls. Randall was obsessed with winning because the prize money and the roads that victory opened would have lifted him out of poverty. But I won, Anna.

"That same day, his girlfriend named Lisa quickly ran over to me. Not because, as Randall thinks, she fell in love with me immediately, but because I had a lot of marijuana in the house. She was completely addicted and ended badly, which Randall blames me for, too, although I did nothing except have sex with her, and in general, I was not interested in her more or less than all the other girls I slept with."

"What happened to her?"

"From marijuana, she jumped to heroin. She overdosed but was saved. As I said, I don't know much about her, Anna. She wasn't my girlfriend. Randall can tell you whatever he wants, but I had nothing to do with this story. I'm not responsible for all the girls I've just slept with."

"Randall said nothing to me, Teo… He just warned me to keep aloof from you. Now I can see why."

"Can see why? How can you, Anna! I don't care what he told you or what he didn't. I have told you all that your lover may have against me. But you can scarcely see that he speaks out of envy. Everything I do and have now, he wanted to have. But whatever depraved life I lead, I deserved that reward, Anna. I was better than him, and I was appreciated."

"Really, let's go out, please," Anna maintained, and silently finishing dressing up, she left the room.

Chapter 63

They rode in silence. Teo stared at the road, and Anna tried to control her thoughts, which seemed to move her from side to side with their amplitude. She wanted to scream, to cry, to laugh.

"Do you feel anything for me?" she blurted out, and Teo slowed down at the suddenness of her question.

"What?"

"Do you feel anything for me? You said you usually just sleep with girls, and you don't care."

"You think I've been lying to you all this time and just wished to sleep with you, Anna?" Teo looked at her, trying to read the emotions on her face.

"I don't know what to think. Though I still think that all of a sudden, you're not likely to fall in love with me."

Teo stopped the auto. Anna looked at him anxiously, expecting drama.

"Why did you stop?"

"We're here." He nodded toward the flashing twenty-four-hours' cafe banner. It was still very early, but this cafe was always happy to serve customers. "I figured we need to eat something."

"Oh. Okay." She opened the car door to go outside, but Teo slammed the door shut.

"Wait," he said softly. "Anna. I didn't lie to you. Never. I know it all looks very fast. Believe me—it is for me, too. But this is my first time, so to say. I never liked any girl before I met you. So, these feelings fell on me like a snowball, and I just couldn't keep quiet. I wanted you to know how I feel about you. I didn't lie to you about anything, Anna."

Anna looked into his eyes. Was he telling the truth? Did it matter whether or not he loved her? Anna admitted to herself feeling some relief when Teo assured her of his feelings. She was looking at him, and she didn't see Randall instead. She saw Teo.

"Turn around. Take me home, please."

"What? We came to the cafe, Anna."

"I throw the dice, as you advised me to do."

"Anna, God, I was furious, I was angry, that's why I..."

"I'm throwing the dice, Teo. I want this. Come what may. But now take me back home, I do not want to eat."

"Anna, you're so bewildering!"

"Teo! Let's go home!"

Teo froze, perplexed. He was so confused that he didn't even know how to act. He glanced at her again, then started the engine and turned toward the house.

***

He was not afraid she might leave him. He was afraid she seemed to be punishing herself for something. She wanted to know if heaven would punish her by tying her to Teo? Would she just leave him because her relationship with him was a mistake?

Deep down, he knew why she was with him. He saw what she was in this relationship for. He knew that he was only an instrument of her despair, of her attempts to reach Randall's heart. But he couldn't "turn on" pride and send her away with her selfishness.

He did love her with all his heart. She thinks he suddenly fell in love with her when she flew back to Milan, and it was impossibly fast, but she was wrong.

He loved her when Randall arrived once, to quarrel with him about tourists, saying that he was expecting a charming chick called Anna Ryans, and he desperately needed money and tourists, and he, Teo, was just the pig that made money hand over the glove, running the market like a monopolist. When Teo joked that if Randall would show how charming this Anna Ryans was, he'd give him and Bernardo a couple of groups of foreigners, but not anymore. And Randall, without a second thought, threw a phone with a girl's photo at Teo. And that was when Teo knew that Anna was the one for whom his heart beat.

Chapter 64

The next day Anna has fallen ill. She was glad to stay in bed, surrounded by the fruit and flowers Teo had brought, as soon as he realized she wasn't feeling well. He had to leave for work that day. After making sure she was all right at home by herself, he drove off.

Left alone, Anna first fell into a deep sleep with chaotic events, and upon awakening, binge-watched the season of "The Ghost Whisperer."

By evening, she had regained her normal state of health and prepared a romantic dinner while she waited for Teo to return from work.

He was very late, but when he arrived, he was genuinely surprised to find Anna in a crimson evening dress, with curled hair, scarlet lipstick on her lips, standing in front of a luxurious dinner, beckoning with its magnificent smell.

"Waiting for who? Confess!" Teo joked, putting off the working overalls.

"For you, silly!" Anna smiled.

"Are you feeling better? You're very beautiful… dressed up."

"I'm almost well." Anna handed him the guitar. "But a couple of songs will completely heal me."

Teo let out a satisfied chuckle and wasted no time in performing Jason Mraz—"I'm Yours," making mind-blowing faces.

"Thanks for everything." When he finished, Teo gestured toward the food table.

"Let's taste it?"

For the next few minutes, the romance faded into the background, and the clatter of plates and spoons began, for both were hungry. Teo looked at Anna with genuine happiness on his face, and she did smile back at him sincerely.

That was a moment of quiet time, when they were together, tet-a-tet, just eating, talking about everything. Anna bore Teo's snide comments about "The Ghost Whisperer" and teased him about his favorite movie, "The Notebook."

That dinner, even after so many years, Anna had replayed in her mind, remembering every detail, every smile, every look they had given each other that night before they had gone to bed and spent a night in each other's arms.

Chapter 65

"**C**an't believe it!"

Anna opened her eyes and looked at Teo anxiously. He had a phone in his hand.

"Teo? What's the matter?"

"Nothing. Randall texted me, that's the matter. He won't give up his silly plan to see you!"

Anna rose from the bed.

"Why are you so nervous? I told you I wanted to see him, to sort out our misunderstanding. It will bring me relief. Stop reacting like that. I'm lying in bed with him or with you, after all! What a *good morning!*"

"Sorry," Teo breathed out, looking down. "Randall is just vexing me. If it weren't for you, I'd have killed him with a shovel."

"Stop talking nonsense, Teo." Anna closed his mouth a light kiss and, stroking his cheek, added, "I'm with you, not with Randall. That should give you some reassurance."

"Yeah." Teo nodded and smiled to change the subject. "Coffee? I still can't get used to you sleeping so long. I'm all twisted up, but I wanted to be sure to be there when you open your eyes."

"Oh, I did open them. With you swearing. I need to know more about your exes, so I have something to be angry about, too!"

"Believe me. I know little about them myself," Teo drawled sarcastically as he was about to leave the room to make coffee.

"Bounce, lover boy!" Anna threw a pillow after him but missed it. They both laughed, and Teo hurried away.

Anna ran to the bathroom, made exceptional makeup, and dressed up again. She felt special.

After an hour of appearance magic, she finally was satisfied and went to look for Teo to be verbally appreciated for the efforts.

"Wow!" he exclaimed as she was turning several times in front of him. "And all this for Randall?"

"Huh? Teo!"

"He's expecting you at the railway station in the afternoon. Apparently, you have some shared memories there."

"You know what, Teo!" Anna pouted. "I dressed up for you, but you ruined everything! What a man you are! And there are no memories of the station!"

Teo smiled sardonically and pulled her closer.

"I know it's for me, silly." He kissed her. "You didn't know you had your date today. But I'm still jealous. Your beauty belongs to me, and this sly one will enjoy it for free."

"It's awful, Teo." Anna melted finally from flattering words. "Where's my coffee, anyway!"

Raising an eyebrow at the impertinence, Teo smiled and handed her a freshly brewed drink that smelled delicious.

They both had a hasty breakfast, as Teo had to go to work. He promised to take Anna to the train station and pick her up on his lunch break.

As they rode in the car, Anna started getting nervous. In the morning, she had been almost irrefutable that she would be perfectly tranquil and unemotional if she met Randall. She knew that she still loved him deep down, but she was determined to let go of those feelings and do what she needed to see Randall.

Having met Teo, she started to let slip the thoughts of revenge. Being with Teo, she seemed to reconsider her pain and would not want now to quarrel nor to try, by all means, to hurt Randall. She knew she was deluding herself by cherishing that hope—that Randall was jealous of some feeling for her and not of the usual ego and hunter instinct of all men.

But now, as she approached the station, she was practically drenched in a nervous sweat. Her hands were shaking, and she tried to hide them from Teo. He was thinking somewhere already at work. However, the real worries were just ahead.

Chapter 66

Anna got out of Teo's car and headed for the platform. She was almost physically ill. She wanted to turn and walk away before Randall saw her.

What was she even doing here? Why see him? What would she gain from it? Did she expect Randall to say he was sorry? What was Teo thinking now, driving to work, leaving her with her ex? Did she want Randall back? Wanted to be with him no matter what? Or maybe she should throw it all away, and the events of her life should be all about Teo, and she did not have to come to the platform to get something out of Randall…

All these thoughts were drowned out by the unmistakable recognition of Randall, leaning against the gigantic palm tree that decorated the station hall. He was talking to someone on the phone, gesturing widely and smiling with all his charm.

He looked as stunning as ever. Other words just don't match, and this opinion was not only of infatuated Anna but of a clear majority of those present at the station of the fair sex, who Ah-ed and Oh-ed when he accidentally fell into their field of vision.

He wore bright blue jeans, a cotton shirt with an oriental pattern, and a stylish man's handkerchief intricately tied around his neck. He was using the phone with one hand, and the other one was… in a cast.

"Randall!" Anna called timidly, and he turned, interrupting his phone conversation.

A genuine smile lit his face, and Anna's heart sank. All her efforts to forget him, to hurt him, to love another man, shattered at the same moment when Randall, recognizing Anna at once, hung up and walked over to her, giving her a warm hug.

"Beautiful!" he whispered. "Hello, my beautiful."

Automatically, she returned his embrace, her common sense forgotten. She wanted to strangle him in that embrace, to cover his pretty face with kisses, to cry out how she loved him, how she missed him, and how hard it was for her to live without him.

"What happened to your arm, Randall?" she asked instead.

"Oh, that? It's nothing special. Broke a wall chatting with you." He laughed. "And smashed the phone. Look, I have a new one!"

He proudly showed Anna the latest model of an iPhone.

"Impressive," the girl smirked.

"Walk?" he suggested, holding out his sane hand.

"Sure."

They left the station, and Anna asked why he decided to meet here.

"You'll see."

Having crossed the road, they turned the corner of a high-rise building and found themselves in the same charming landscape park called Sempione—the attraction, which began their adventures together.

"I can't believe it!" Anna gasped, tears welling in her eyes. "We…"

"Yes!" Randall smiled, wiping away her tears. "Yes!"

Again they walked the familiar paths. Randall again came up with historical dates and humorous memories of Milan's famous places, forcing Anna to continuously laugh and be distracted from the only feeling that hunted her, which was the pain.

They went to the same cafe with the surly Arab proprietor, where they were on the first day of her arrival, strolled through Milan's quiet and main streets, talked about Italy, local customs, Randall's favorite politics topics, and other life's moments. She found out that Randall took the time to see his family in Austria and returned to university. Asking about Bernardo, she learned that he was also studying and that in a couple of months, they planned to go to China to travel.

Dusked. They walked for a long time, and the girl just had no strength anymore to gaze at all these painfully familiar places.

"Shall we sit down?" she suggested, seeing a vacant bench in a deserted playground.

Randall, glancing at her, saw that the time came to change the subject. He reluctantly sat down on the bench, inviting Anna to sit on his lap, assuring her that the bench was freezing and that was the only reason she should be in his arms.

"Randall," she began, "we need to talk."

"Yes, Anna, I know, we do. But I don't know how to talk about anything exactly or what the right phrases are."

"Neither do I," Anna admitted. "But I didn't come to fight. I came to ask you."

"What do you want to ask?" his face dropped, and he began to draw intricate patterns in the sand with the toe of his sneaker to hide his nerves.

"How could you?"

"Uff. I wish you wouldn't put it that way. But what can I say? I thought we were friends, Anna. I didn't think we were a couple. I understand that you're asking me specifically about having some fun with that girl, but I didn't feel like I was doing anything bad."

"Bad?"

"Something that could hurt you. I never meant to hurt you, Anna. You're a wonderful girl, smart, beautiful, honest, sophisticated, and an amazing friend."

Anna cringed at the last sentence but said nothing. Her eyes glistened with tears, and he stroked her hair, trying to calm her.

"How was it?" Anna asked suddenly.

"How was what?"

"That *fun*. Did you enjoy it? Was she pretty? Better than me? What's wrong with me, Randall?"

"Shhh, beautiful. Calm down now, and don't talk nonsense. You're gorgeous. In everything. It was nothing. I just slept with some girl at a party, that's all."

"How was it?" Anna insisted.

Randall shivered but answered:

"There was a random party. We danced, she started kissing my neck, harassing me. We found a room, and we did it. That's all, Anna. End of story. No, I don't love her, anticipating your silly thoughts. Yes, she was beautiful, but not as perfectly beautiful as you."

"Then why? I don't understand, Randall. You're a hypocrite. You knew I loved you, and I told you that! Why did you do that? We weren't friends, Randall! Friends don't sleep with each other!"

Traitorous tears flowed in a stream, and pride left her. She clung to Randall and cried on his shoulder.

"I'm sorry, beautiful. Please forgive me," he whispered, trying in vain to calm her.

He managed with difficulty to soothe her sobs. To lighten the mood, he suggested going to the pastry shop to buy some nice vegetarian dessert to smile finally.

Sniffling, Anna went into the tiny pastry shop near the playground where they had been all this time. Randall bought two freshly squeezed orange juices and two veggie cakes.

They perched on high chairs and sat close together, so they could talk over the unbearable noise the other visitors made with their animated conversations and discussions in Italian.

"So, you're with Teo now," Randall stated, chewing on his cake.

Anna glanced at him, trying to read his mood. He looked calm. She'd imagined this moment so many times. When she'd thrown Randall to the face that she was now with Teo, the one he hated, that she was sleeping with him and would always be with him.

But in reality, all her emotions were turned upside down. She wished she'd never met Teo, wished she'd never stayed with him, so she could say she'd just been alone all along and never wanted to hurt him. All her plans for retaliation had vanished the moment she saw Randall. Now she didn't want to rewrite the story with him. She wanted to delete the story with Teo.

"I suppose so," she answered.

"Mm."

"He's a good guy. He's very kind to me, and..."

"Did you sleep with him?"

"What?"

"Did you sleep with him?"

Anna gulped. Randall looked into her eyes and grasped the answer.

Chapter 67

"Anna..." he muttered, shaking his head as if he could not believe it. "I'm speechless. What for? Why, Anna??"

"I... I don't know."

"Do you love him?"

"No, I..."

"Then why did you do that? Why are you with him, Anna? Teo's a dangerous guy. He's a terrible person, Anna. You know nothing about him."

Anticipating the conversation, Anna decided that she would lose in covering what Teo had said about their mutual aversion and how she was on his side anyway. So she decided that they should ask for the bill because it was too late.

When they had paid, they went out into the street and stopped. Anna looked at Randall. There was no pain in his face, only a kind of disappointment.

"He'll pick you up?" he asked coldly.

"Yes," Anna replied. "Teo asked you to call him when we're done..."

"... sorting things out," he finished her sentence sadly. "Anna, don't go back to him. Call him and tell that you're not coming back."

"What? Randall, are you out of your mind? I have everything in Teo's house. Why shouldn't I come back? Where should I be?"

"You will stay in my place. I'll pick you up. Don't go back to him, Anna. He's a bad man, and he's deceiving you."

"In what way is he deceiving me, Randall? In all the time I've known Teo, he's never lied to me. He treats me well, and he loves me!"

"*Loves* you!? Teo never loved anyone. He is an unfeeling machine, focused only on making money!"

It seemed that this conversation would not be avoided after all.

"Randall, enough. I don't think so, and I don't want to discuss Teo behind his back."

"What did he tell you? That I'm bad, and he's the good one? Right?"

"He didn't say that."

"What did he tell you?"

"That you abhorred him after you lost a music contest, and your girlfriend ran over to him."

Randall snorted.

"Ran over? He forced her! He needs to get his hands on everything that should belong to me!"

"Randall, you're being immature."

"Really? Did he mention how he drugged Liz, how she ended up in the hospital? How he never even visited her and never even talked to her again?"

"I don't know the details of the story. It's all unfortunate, and I honestly don't want to go into all this."

"How can you say that? How can you be around a man like that, knowing what he's done to my life?"

"What do you want me to do, Randall?"

"I want you to take your things and leave him once and for all."

"Why would I do that?"

Anna waited for him to say that her relationship with Teo was a mistake, that Randall knew he loved her, that he wanted to start over. She prayed he would say something like that.

"Because Teo's a bird of bad omen, and I fret about you, Anna. I'll call him right now and tell him to return your things because you're not going back to this villa." With a quick movement of his free hand, Randall pulled the phone out of his pocket to dial Teo's number.

"Randall, don't be presumptuous! Don't call him." She swallowed, realizing that her forlorn hope had vanished. "I'm going to Teo's."

"Anna!" shouted Randall in rage. "Why are you doing this?! You want to hurt me by being with a man I hate for everything he's done to me in my life! He took the life that was meant for me. He's not the one who should be flinging money in all directions. I am! Lizzie wasn't supposed to be with him. She was supposed to be with me!"

The phone rang. It was Teo. Randall passed it to Anna, and she answered. He asked if he and Randall had finished their "date" because he was passing the station and wanted to take her home.

"Yes, we're done," Anna mumbled, trying to calm down. "I'm ready to go home."

There was so much pain on Randall's face at that moment that Anna's heart sank. But she realized that his pain had nothing to do with her, that it was not his feelings for her that hurt him, but because, despite his pleas, she was going with Teo, and that was the only thing that hurt him.

"I'll walk you out!" Randall barked, turning toward the station.

Chapter 68

They had to stand in silence for about ten minutes before Teo's car finally appeared on the horizon.

Teo got out of the BMW and dashed toward the couple. At the same moment, from nowhere, Bernardo appeared and, shaking hands with Randall, fell on Anna with wild cries of joy and embraces. Anna was happy to see him, but he riveted her attention only on one point that chilled her blood.

Teo was walking towards Randall.

"Anna! How beautiful you are!! How good to see you! We parted not so long ago, but it seemed an eternity!" Bernardo exclaimed, clasping her in his arms.

"I'm glad, too!" Anna said, watching the state of events with horror.

Teo walked over to Randall and motioned him aside, nodding to Bernardo and Anna in greeting.

"What will they do?" screamed Anna.

"Relax, Anna. They've known each other for years. They may be enemies, but they have nothing to fight about. They're brainless," smiled Bernardo.

Teo hinted to Anna to get in the car.

"Bernardo!" Anna roared and rushed herself into the arms of the guy. "Bernardo, I love Randall! God, help me, what to do! I don't want to be with Teo!"

"Anna, what are you talking about?"

"I love Randall, Bernardo!"

"And he loves you, too?"

"He doesn't love me, Bernardo! He *doesn't* love me, Bernardo! Oh, my God!" cried the girl, unsteady on her feet from the convulsive wailing. "I don't want to be with Teo!"

"Oh, Anna!" Bernardo exhaled.

After talking for quite some time, Teo and Randall walked over to them, and Anna threw her arms around Randall.

"Randall, please, I love you, Randall!" Anna screamed, losing control over herself, her hands around Randall's neck. "Randall, please, I don't love him!"

"Let's go home, Anna." Teo tried to pull her away from Randall, but she refused to obey. "Anna, let go of him. Go get in the car."

"I don't want to be with him, Randall! I love only you!!!"

"Anna, you have to go…" Randall said, trying to free himself from the girl's grip. "Go with him, Anna."

"What? No! Don't say that, Randall! Please, do not leave me!" the pain of his words seemed to paralyze her.

"Anna, you have to go…" Randall repeated.

"No! No!"

"Come, Anna." Teo finally pulled her away from Randall. "Don't make a scene in public."

"Randall!… No!" she cried as Teo dragged her toward the car.

Randall just stared after her. He had nothing to say to her.

Teo shoved her into the backseat of the car and spoke sympathetically:

"Don't humiliate yourself like that, Anna. You can see he doesn't love you."

Anna said no more but kept looking toward Randall, who was leaving the platform with Bernardo.

Nothing ever hurt her that much.

"Here." Teo handed her the rose. "I bought it on the way home from work. Thought you'd like it."

Without another word, he walked around the car and got behind the wheel, starting the engine.

Nothing ever hurt him that much.

Chapter 69

They drove in silence. Teo knew that if either of them said a word, there would be an explosion. And he wasn't sure he could control his emotions right now.

He kept replaying the conversation scene with Randall in his mind when he came up to him on the platform while Anna was talking to Bernardo.

***

"Hi."

"Hello again, Teo."

"I came to get the girl."

"Not for the first time."

"Huh?"

"I said it's not the first time you've come to get the girl," Randall said with a bitter grin.

Teo's eyes flashed.

"It's not the first time you've screwed up so much that people who truly love you run out of your life."

"Really. You're an angel. Rich and famous. How could anyone not love you?"

"Randall, you're ridiculous."

"Anna's not going anywhere with you, Teo. I want her to stay with me. Be a man, and without any scandals, just bring her things and documents."

Teo smiled and answered:

"You want? What does Anna want? Listen to me carefully, Randall. We both know you don't love her, and before you took her down the notch with your childish adventures, you better shut your mouth right now.

Anna's coming with me, and if you try to stop me in any way, I'll turn your face to mush right here. You feel me?"

Randall was about to pounce on Teo, but they both looked at Anna, who was being crushed in Bernardo's arms, and restrained themselves.

"Don't humiliate her with your behavior, Randall."

"Poor Teo, you don't know what to do to make her notice you—neither the songs nor the money help, huh? I bet it makes you sick to think that she loves me, such a poor, simple fellow."

Teo grabbed Randall's arm, careful not to let the audience see, and said:

"Listen, you poor, simple fellow. I have absolutely no interest in what you're talking about, but I'm warning you that today is the last time you're gonna mess with my relationship with Anna. Stay away from me if you value your teeth."

"She loves *me*," Randall said through his teeth. "You can't change that, no matter how much you threaten. Just remember, you can't force yourself to be loved."

"You selfish! Look at her! What can you give her? You don't feel anything for her, and that's just low. Let her go. She deserves better. At least act like her real friend. You tell her you're *friends*, right?"

With that, he let go of Randall's cast, and they both went to Anna and Bernardo.

Teo pulled up outside the house and, as Anna got out of the car, started the engine and drove off in an unknown direction.

Chapter 70

Anna waited until morning, but Teo did not come until the following night. He reeked of alcohol. Without a word to the agitated girl, he undressed and went to bed.

Anna wanted to talk to him, but she didn't know what to say. Her quenched eyes betrayed only the pain for Randall, and she was sure that all the words, if she opened her mouth, would be about him.

Still, she was mortified by the way she treated Teo, the way she'd made a scene on the platform, hugging Randall and screaming of her affection.

She knew everyone had heard everything. She knew she had caused Teo an unbearable affliction. But what could she do? How to change the intentions of the heart? She tried her best to banish him from her heart. But she still doted on Randall. Even after he told her to sod off, she continued to love him despite all.

She was not ashamed that she beseeched Randall not to leave her, that she shouted all over the street she loved him. If the entire world had been listening to them at that moment, she would still have screamed that she loved him and begged him not to leave…

Even knowing he didn't love her back.

"Why?" Teo's voice broke into her thoughts.

"What?"

"Why, Anna?"

"Teo, I"

Teo swung around to face her and looked her straight in the eyes as he fought his way through the gloom.

"Why do you bestow your heart on someone who treats it like it's trash?"

"Teo"

"Why am I not worthy of cherishing your heart, Anna?"

Anna covered her face with her hands. She would not cry anymore. For all the hours she had been home alone, she seemed to have cried a river. But she couldn't look into Teo's sincere eyes, even through the night, knowing that whatever she said would only hurt him.

Teo sighed heavily and said:

"But you must know that I will still love you. Even after you yelled at the world that you didn't love me and you dispatched me out. Even after every time you trampled me in the mud. Even after I let you go. I love you, Anna, no matter what, and you always remember that. And I expect nothing in return. I'm just telling you to know that. I love you, and that's why I'm letting you go. I will no longer hold you in the shackles of this hateful union. Forgive me if I have unwittingly led you astray from the path your heart desires to follow. Just mind this—he doesn't love you, Anna."

With that, Teo looked once more into Anna's tearful eyes with anguish, smiled sadly, and turned away to sleep.

Chapter 71

"Where do I go, where do I go…" muttered the girl, making her way through the enormous snowdrifts.

Stepfather threw her out at dawn. It was winter. It was so cold that even breathing brought unbearable pain from the thin icy air in the morning.

She moped around to find some shelter and wait until morning to try again to enter the home and see if her stepdad had fallen asleep. All her books were in the house. Before going to school, she wanted to take the backpack, at least, if the usurper was still awake. For now, all she could do was wait.

Having reached an abandoned barn, she decided it would be warmer inside than outside. When she opened the rickety door, which creaked with oil-free screws, she was glad to find that there was no one in. Hobos or groups of freezing homeless animals usually inhabited such places.

She dropped into a corner and curled up, whispering a prayer of thanks, and fell asleep.

After a while, there was a rustle. As Anna opened her eyes, she saw her stepfather standing over her with an ax he was swinging to strike.

She screamed and…

She woke up.

Her breath caught in her throat, and her eyes filled with terror. She automatically turned to Teo, leaning over her with an expression of compassion and pain on his face.

"Another nightmare," he said, more in the affirmative than expecting an answer.

"Teo, I dreamed he wanted to kill me," Anna murmured, still trembling.

"Who is he?"

"Varrel. My stepfather."

"Did he try to kill you in reality?"

"No, he... He could never. He's a terrible man, but he wouldn't kill me, would he? Right, Teo? He's too weak for that. Teo?"

Teo sighed sadly and tried to comfort her by taking her in his arms. It was hard for him to understand what she was talking about because she mentioned nothing about her family. He knew that sometimes it was just superfluous.

Anna clung to his shoulders and held him tightly. She thought only she and Teo existed in the world now. She was so terrified that she couldn't think of anything to say about what was happening to her.

At last, gathering her wits and moving a little away from the hideous dream, she explained:

"My stepfather expressed an insuperable aversion to me and treated me terribly. I've learned to ignore that part of my life. In reality, I only stick to the positive side of things, but his words, his moves, his actions haunt my dreams, and there's nothing I can do. He reminds me that I am nobody, worthy only of defiance, no matter what I do. I am incapable of anything and need to remember that above that level I will not go, I..."

"Shush," Teo closed her mouth with a kiss. "Don't prattle that evil. You're not nobody. You're the most beautiful girl in the world, and you drive everyone crazy with your beauty. Look what cockfights are happening because of you!"

Anna forced a smile and faded again.

"Thanks for the support, Teo. But I know what I am. Very nice of you"

"Your stepdad is a low-life. I can see he's ruined your life and your self-esteem, but you know what? I'm not going to give you a 'love yourself so others will love you' speech. I already love you, despite all the horrible thoughts and labels you've put on yourself because of that Varnall."

"Varrel."

"Yeah, right. Whatever name they gave him at birth, they had to stop at the word *low-life*."

He showered her with encouraging kisses and offered to go to the kitchen to find some mineral water for his hangover and something to cheer her up.

She nodded, and they headed for the kitchen. As soon as they sat at the table, Anna said:

"I'm sorry about everything, Teo."

"Let's not talk about it, Ann."

"Forgive me."

He looked away, pretending to look for something to eat in the refrigerator.

"I am truly sorry, Teo…"

Anna caught her breath and looked at Teo, expecting to see anger or disappointment. But his face was impossible to understand. It was like a stone and expressed nothing.

"Teo, I just"

"It's all right, Anna."

"I'll give you some time alone."

"Certainly."

She went out of the kitchen, hiding her tears.

Teo sank into a chair and closed his eyes, thinking even if she ever loved him, he would be the happiest man on the planet.

But fate always has its plans.

"Is this the end" he rhetorically uttered in a whisper and buried his face in his hands.

Chapter 72

Leaving the room, Anna found Teo already on the balcony. He was smoking and playing some melancholy chords on his guitar.

"Teo," she started, "you are so hurt"

He looked at her and grinned.

"If you're looking for confirmation of your idea that I maliciously planned our relationship and am now upset that it didn't work out, then you're not gonna get it. I'm not upset that you feel nothing for me, Anna."

"You're mad at me. I can see that."

"I'm not mad at you, Anna. I'm mad at everything. You're leaving in a couple of days, and I don't think we'll see each other again. That hurts me because I know your mind is full of Randall, and your time with me is dust to you."

"Teo, please don't say that!" she pleaded, falling into his arms. "Please forgive me for all the words I shouted on the platform."

"You don't regret saying them, Anna," Teo said calmly, pulling away from her. "All those words were true, so do not retract. And it only hurts more. But I just can't comprehend *how* you can love him. He's a dog in the manger, Anna."

"Teo, Teo!" Anna hugged him again, holding him. "I'm here with you. I'm not with him, Teo."

"It's true," he sighed heavily, "but you only came with me because he sent you off. That's why. Otherwise, you would have agreed to run away with Randall. Even though he just couldn't stand the idea of you with me. Even seeing that he doesn't love you, you're still willing to blind yourself to any idea that allows you to be around him. But know this, Anna, it won't do you any good."

Teo pulled away from her grip and stood up, lighting another cigarette.

"Teo, I am asking, let us not part like that. You just reminded me I am leaving soon. If the last hours you are determined to hate me, I cannot take it!"

"Silly Anna!" He shook his head. "Your empty head will never understand the depth of my feelings. You will always try to ascribe to me what is not. It doesn't matter what you do or say, Anna. I don't hate you. I love you."

Teo tossed his half-smoked cigarette angrily and looked at her.

She was silent, her eyes downcast.

"You're right," he said in a calm tone. "We have a little time. Let us have some fun?"

Anna nodded shyly as she met his gaze.

"I suggest walking along the waterfront and visiting Burton restaurant in Porta Nuova."

"Is it good?"

"Oh, it is. Delicious food there." He smiled and added, "And it's posh."

"Very, very posh?"

"Very, very posh. But for me, it's nothing," he winked.

Anna finally laughed. As soon as she saw Teo lose his guard, she leaped back into his arms. He couldn't help laughing, too.

"Come on, put on something gorgeous."

"You're not working today?"

"No, and I'm starving."

"All I have is the black dress and the one I wore when you and I had a romantic dinner. Will that do?"

"No more outfits?"

"No."

"Just get in the car. We're going shopping. And then, finally, some breakfast. I'll dress up, too."

Startled, Anna hurried to her car. She was glad they'd talked and tried not to think about how bad things really were. The realization that she had tickets back to Mining Great City hit her with a force that made her ears ring. She knew that she would never see Randall again, contrary to Teo's opinion, that she would now communicate only with Randall. Brooding over the scene at the station repeatedly, each time she heard Randall calmly saying, *"Anna, you have to go."* The words stabbed her in the heart like a dagger each time, and feelings of deep vexation and irrevocable despair choked her throat.

She knew she couldn't make him feel anything for her. She had to get Randall out of her life, out of her heart, out of her mind. But how?...

Chapter 73

They pulled into some local fashion boutiques and went shopping. Teo enjoyed picking out tons of different dresses for Anna, loading up on a skinny, sleep-deprived salesman named Chuck. She laughed and clapped her hands over every new dress Teo put on the poor assistant.

Chuck, swaying under the weight of potential purchases, obediently followed the couple into the dressing room and was inexpressibly glad to get rid of the burden, even expecting a sickly percentage of the possible proceeds.

Teo gestured to the leather seat opposite the fitting room.

"And you will parade in front of me in all these wonderful dresses so we can choose beautiful options!"

"Like in the movie 'Pretty woman!'" Anna giggled.

"Like in the movie 'Pretty woman.'" Teo nodded and stretched out in his chair, turning on the MP3 player.

"I'll put on the music!" snatching the device from him, the girl laughed.

"Hey! I want to put on the soundtrack of the movie!" Teo smiled as he wrestled with the girl, but he lost, and the player ended up in her frail hands.

"Ta-da!" Anna exclaimed sarcastically. "Now sit down and wait for me to come out!"

Brenton Wood's 1967 song "Oogum Boogum" started playing, and Teo couldn't help but laugh. Anna stepped out from behind the screen in the most seductive way, showing off a chic blue ruffle dress that Teo immediately brushed aside, sending her for the next one. Enjoying a few more choices in the most mind-blowing colors and designs, he approved of a champagne cocktail dress when Ellie Goulding's "Love Me Like You Do" was already playing. Anna was effectively spinning in front of him, forcing him to lower an embarrassed look, hiding genuine admiration.

"Decided," she whispered in his ear and kissed him on the lips, embarrassing him to the point of blushing.

Later in the evening, they were strolling quietly along the avenues. Ricardo and Leticia were glad to accompany them.

The air on the quay was fresh and breezy, and the vendors of trinkets and other souvenirs were eager to sell.

Anna held Teo's hand and tried unsuccessfully to read the emotion on his face. He had always been such a mystery. Now she needed to know what he was thinking, and she didn't have the heart to ask.

"Here we are!" Teo said proudly as they approached the luxurious Burton restaurant in the futuristic Port Nuova neighborhood. "My treat!"

They entered a chic room with an ultra-modern design, executed in a minimalist manner with Italy's inherent elegance. Ricardo involuntarily gasped, and the girls hurried to take the most beautifully decorated table. Teo had obviously been to this place more than once. The waiters knew him, and several of the visitors asked for his autograph.

"I'm so glad you're rich and famous," Ricardo said enthusiastically. "Thanks to you, we can go to such luxurious places for free!"

Everyone laughed and began to choose dishes from the menu. Teo was relaxed and advised friends of things he has tried in previous visits. For Anna, he and the waiter for a long time have been choosing the best vegetarian dish. Anna was very pleased with Teo's tender attitude, attention to the smallest details of her life. She watched admiringly as he explained to a waiter she knew that Anna liked this sauce, not the other, that the chef always added meat, and she didn't eat meat. He asked the drink to be necessarily so-and-so, the first dish so-and-so, the second one so-and-so.

"Thank you," she whispered in his ear, and he beamed.

Over dinner, the atmosphere of tension seemed to dissolve completely. Teo was having a lively discussion with Ri in Italian, and the girls were discussing the latest fashion trends and the guys themselves.

"You're so lucky!" delightedly mumbled Leticia. "Teo is a rare gem, and he seems to breathe you!"

"Thank you," Anna murmured, looking away.

"You're a wonderful couple that nothing can break."

Anna looked at Teo and nodded at Leticia.

"I guess so," she drawled. "Nothing indeed."

Chapter 74

They came home together, exhausted. The guys decided to have a little beer and play computer games, and the girls just shut themselves in the room to gossip and have fun.

Leticia dressed up in one or the other of the dresses Teo had bought for Anna.

"I envy you so much!!" she exclaimed admiringly. "You don't even know what card you've drawn! Teo is amazing!"

"Well, well, I shall soon be jealous!" Anna joked. "Ricardo's a great guy, too, Leti."

"Yes, of course, but not so rich and famous. Look what happens when Teo goes out in public! He's harassed! I am sure that soon he will become a world-famous DJ! And you will bask in his success!"

Anna laughed, trying this way to change the subject, and showered Leticia with dresses. Her gaze fell on the phone on the nightstand.

No. Don't even think about it. Literally, all the internal organs seemed to scream to her.

Just for a second! was her inevitable answer.

"I'm going to the bathroom!" Anna blurted to Leticia, who hadn't even heard the remark.

Grabbing the phone from the table, Anna slipped into the bathroom and locked the door.

Teo never locked his device, so she logged in to her social network account and discovered four messages from Randall.

Opening chat, she saw a video and a long text from him. Without hesitation, she hit the "Play" button.

It was the video from a music competition, from which the mutual aversion of the guys rooted. Anna watched with a sinking heart as Randall played an unknown composition on the guitar and sang. He had a great voice and enjoyed the performance. Anna had never heard him play. She hadn't even known that he could, until the latest events, so it was a real shock to see him on stage with a guitar, in an expensive suit, with his hair lacquered.

After that, there were some other two performers, and lastly, Teo came on stage. He wore a simple T-shirt and jeans, his messy hair completing the style. As he commenced, the entire audience and jury froze. He performed a lyrical ballad of his own composition and played as Anna had never seen him play. He literally was the music. He was all the words of the song, all the chords, all the pauses. He merged with the Universe itself, and no one had any doubt that he was worthy of victory. He was excellent. When he finished the song, he just smiled and jumped off the stage to enthusiastic gasps.

The depth of Teo's talent shocked Anna. Although Randall also played beautifully, the difference would have been apparent even to a deaf person. And yet, it puzzled her why Randall had sent the video. The lengthy message was supposed to explain everything to her, so she began to read.

"Anna, here's a video from my performance that made Teo and me eternal enemies. I hope you see now that I was worthy of victory and not him."

Anna sighed sadly, shaking her head. Text followed:

"But that's not why I'm writing to you, though. I haven't been able to sleep since we parted on the platform. I keep replaying all the moments in my head. You are in my head all the time, and I see that I have missed something fundamental. I think about you every second, and the picture of Teo pushing you into the car doesn't go out of my head. I thought I was doing the right thing, that you'd be better off with him, that he was a good match for you. But I just can't accept it. Every second I think that not he should run hand in your hair and kiss you, but me. Not he should walk with you in Milan, but me. Not he is your fate, but I am. I think I know what I missed, Anna. I think I love you, Anna. Do you hear me? I love you, and I want you with me, not him."

Anna froze on the last two sentences and stared at them for several minutes. She read them repeatedly, thinking it was a system failure, some mistake, or maybe it wasn't Randall, or maybe she wasn't Anna, or maybe it wasn't planet Earth.

But no.

"I think I love you, Anna. Do you hear me? I love you, and I want you with me, not him."

Randall wrote it. And she was Anna. And it was planet Earth. And this message was for her.

And Randall was online.

Tears came into her eyes and, wiping them with genuine anger, she wrote:

"How dare you, Randall!"

He answered at once:

"But I love you, and I want us to be together."

"How do you even have the guts to tell me that?"

"It's true. And I'm glad I figured it out before it's too late. I love you!"

"Stop it!"

"I love you! I love you!"

Anna couldn't believe her eyes. Her heart was jubilant, her brain was so angry, her soul so disappointed, and her intuition so anxious. Unable to withstand such an influx of emotions, she logged out abruptly, turned off the phone, and rushed back to the bedroom, where Leticia did not lose her at all. Then she fell on the bed and cried aloud.

Chapter 75

"Anna, dear. Don't be so upset," Leticia murmured anxiously. "What happened? Stop crying, tell me! I can't look at you like that without understanding anything!"

"It's okay, Leti. Leave me for a while, go sit with the boys. I'll come out to you soon," the only thing Anna could mutter in response.

Leticia, after a moment's hesitation, obeyed and left the room. Anna was alone with her thoughts. She tried to sift despair from hope. Randall... How she had waited for that simple phrase and gone to such lengths to hear it. Did he mean what he wrote?

Closing her eyes, Anna seemed to read the messages over and over again. She tried to figure out where the mistake was, what was wrong. Those were the most welcome words of her life, but when she finally got Randall's confession, she didn't feel that relieved.

She dreamed that if he told her he loved her, everything would finally fall into place, they would be together again, and the story would have a happy ending.

The reality was that the confession didn't ease the pain of his cheating, that Teo and his story with Anna didn't just disappear like a second's worth of memories, that the awaited phrase didn't restore her pride and peace, and she didn't rush her back into Randall's arms.

She could not find an explanation for the reaction. But she felt this wild, unbridled joy, this misplaced exultation, this sort of triumph that she had got her way.

"What's to be done about it?" A voice called from the doorway.

"Huh?" the question took Anna aback.

"Attires." Teo nodded toward the scattered dresses and was horrified to see that Anna's eyes were red. "Are you crying?"

"No, no, Teo. I just—I just" no quick answer came to mind. "I was just washing off my make-up. Then I got a little distracted, that's all. I will wash it off quickly and come out to you. I'm just tired of wearing false eyelashes all day."

Deciding that the excuse had worked and not daring to subject Teo's reaction to scrutiny, she slipped into the bathroom and turned on the water as loudly as she could.

"Ay, no! Phone!" she slapped her forehead and, hastily washing off the last of her makeup after a long sob, ran out to shower Teo with more explanations.

He was standing at the door, and as soon as she came out, he motioned her into the hall. He had a phone in his hand.

Anna swallowed, expecting a scandal.

Chapter 76

They went out into the hall, where Ricardo and Leticia were chatting. Teo smiled and flopped down on the sofa, inviting Anna to sit beside him. A little embarrassed by his mood change, Anna hurried to join him so as not to aggravate his temper.

"How about some music?" Ri wondered.

"Marvellous idea!" Leticia clapped her hands.

The guy jumped to adjust the speakers and look for suitable compositions for fun.

In a couple of minutes, a bright salsa rattled, to which Ricardo and Leticia spun in the dance to the lyrical dialogues of Malu Trevejo's "Hasta Luego." Teo suddenly jumped up to dance with them. Anna could not help laughing at their merriment until they dragged her to the center of the room to dance together.

And it was a wonderful moment. Teo danced to the male lead, and then Anna took hers. They looked so happy and harmonious. Any outsider would have given the clear verdict that they made a great couple.

When he was gloomy, her sun shone on him. When Anna herself was lost in dark thoughts, Teo found every opportunity to make her happy again. And now he wasn't even going to argue. He was just enjoying the time they had left to spend together.

It was a night full of dancing until morning, unrestrained fun, and the constant ringing of the telephone on the dresser which drowned the sound of the pouring music.

Randall never heard Anna's voice that night.

Chapter 77

Anna woke up with a terrible headache. Loud music until the morning caused her migraine. It needed no alcohol to understand the hangover of a person on the morning after the party. However, she set her alarm for 7:00 a.m. to spend maximum time with the guys before she flew away. It was her last day in Milan, and the 4:00 p.m. flight reminder was instantly depressing.

Teo was not in the room. Anna hurriedly dressed, applied exquisite makeup to cover the fatigue, and went in search of him.

He was outside with Ricardo in a mock fight. Leticia was arranging food on an open table. As soon as she saw Anna, who was still looking slumberous, began to cheer:

"Good morning! You're so scary-looking! Come for breakfast!"

"Thank you, Leti. You know how to support. A real friend," Anna joked.

"Stop fighting, y'all!" Leticia attempted to separate the boxers. "Like little children, really!"

Teo and Ri pulled away after a good battle, sweating and puffing, and walked over to the table. Teo beamed as Anna stood up:

"Up so early?"

"Today is an exception! I want to spend as much time with you as possible. I mean, all of you," Anna admitted.

"Cute!" Ricardo nodded, hugging both ladies at once.

The company began to eat. They talked about Anna's plans because, most likely, she has been axed. In her heart, Anna laughed it off, although she believed that she expected only good-old-friend unemployment.

Teo was in good spirits, joking a lot and trying to keep everyone positive. But the general mood showed sadness at Anna's departure. Ricardo was worried about Teo, Leticia was concerned about Anna. And the four of them had become superb friends during Anna's time in Milan.

"So, are you ready for it?" Teo asked. "There might be traffic."

Anna nodded weakly. There was an undercurrent in everything. A sense of strange deplorable ignorance made her uneasy. She finished her meal, thanked Leti for her concern, and, having hugged Teo and Ricardo, went to the house's bedroom to pack her suitcase.

As she was busily engaged in arranging her clothes, there was a knock at the door. It was Ricardo.

"Anna," he began.

"Yes?"

Randall called.

"What? Whom?" Anna shivered.

"Now to me. At first, he'd been bugging Teo all day and been carefully sent away. But he had the nerve to call my phone, too."

"What did he want?"

"What do you think? To talk to you! But I told him to forget you, that you're happy with Teo, and that you're leaving back home today anyway, so you're not up to his dramas right now."

Anna gasped at Ricardo's answer.

"Nice. Thanks, Ri."

"Nice?"

"Yes. You said it perfectly. Even too gently. You should have sent him away."

Ricardo frowned incredulously.

"Anna, is that you?"

"It's me, me," the girl smiled. "I can't be a venturesome fool forever."

"That's what I like to hear! That's my Anna!" Ricardo beamed, hugging her. "You deserve the best treatment for such a pretty face!"

Teo came into the room.

"So, here you are, touching my girl!" he jokingly lashed out with his fists on Ricardo. "Hands off!"

Again the battle began. In the process, they crumpled and messed up all things Anna prepared for packing. She fiercely joined the scramble to give them a good dressing-down. Leticia came in with a pot of spaghetti and, realizing she was wasting precious time, threw herself on top of them all, rewarding them with a generous shower of pasta.

And they say too much laughter leads to tears...

Chapter 78

Everyone had to retake a shower, and they moved out of the house late enough to risk being late for the check-in. Anna worried and complained that she wouldn't catch the plane. Teo reassured her that there were no unsolvable problems and that if she missed that plane, he would buy her a ticket for the next one, just not to make him nervous.

Ricardo and Leticia sat in the backseat, singing songs to ease the tension. Anna looked around, trying to remember once again all the streets, cafes, and pavements. Milan was in a turmoil of the day, and the company got into a traffic jam. They kept calm by singing to the guitar, and for the sake of it, Teo and Ricardo had to swap seats.

Finally, having reached the airport, Anna, Teo, Ricardo, and Leticia, in the style of a running late family scene from the movie "Home Alone," rushed to the registration desk and took place in the queue that seemed endless.

"See, you're not alone." Teo grinned, handing her a purse.

"Indeed!" Anna gasped, fixing her clothes and hair. "I'm all wet from sweat!"

"Mm," Teo said, hinting.

Anna hit him with her purse and smiled.

"That's not what you're thinking, young man."

"We're going for a smoke, okay?" Ricardo said, hugging Anna just in case.

"Hey, bro, don't stay too long. This line will pass quickly," Teo said disapprovingly.

"Don't worry, man. We will be fast."

Ricardo and Leticia did not smoke fast, though. Anna drooped. She realized that they would be late and she might not say goodbye to them.

The thought made her angry and disappointed. They were both so dear to her.

"I don't understand why it was impossible just to wait a bit!" Anna protested with annoyance.

"Relax, they're coming," Teo tried to reassure her. "I'll walk you to the end."

They walked down the long corridor, and Teo was in vain trying to reassure her that Ri and Leti were coming, but something had happened that no one could have imagined…

Chapter 79

From behind came a calling cry, "Anna!" and the couple turned. What a shock it was to both of them to see Randall running toward them.

"I can't believe it!" Teo hissed. "What in the world?"

Randall kept shouting, "Anna, Anna!" making his way through the crowd of people.

It stunned Anna. She had expected everything from today, but not this. She watched Randall coming toward her, waving his arms, afraid she wouldn't see him, and her blood ran cold. She couldn't even look at Teo. A private fear had wholly paralyzed her.

"Anna!" Randall finally ran up to her, ignoring Teo completely. "Anna, dear, forgive me, I beg you, I beg you, forgive me! I was blind. I was just blind. I love you! I've always loved you. I just didn't realize it before! Anna!"

"Randall, get out of here!" Teo snarled, tugging at his shoulder, but Randall pulled him back and dropped to his knees in front of Anna.

The crowd gasped, and Anna recoiled in horror.

"Anna, listen to me. I don't care anymore. I've been looking for you all day. I tortured the informants at the front desk to find your flight, I found you, and now I want you to look me in the eye and forgive me. I love you. Look at me!"

"Randall, for God's sake!" Anna gasped, at last, looking around anxiously. People whispered right and left and converged around them in a ring. "Randall, get up now, please! Everyone's looking at us!"

Teo spat in disgust. Anna blushed and tried to comprehend what to do.

"I'll go to smoke, and I'll give you a minute, Anna," Teo said. "When I come back, this circus will be over."

And he strode out of the corridor.

"Teo!" Anna shouted after him, but her eyes fell back on Randall.

She had never seen him like this. He was shaking. He didn't care that people were crowding around and asking each other what the drama was about. His eyes were red with tears and glistened, dropping the new ones.

"Anna, look at me. I can't live if you don't forgive me and come back to me. I know you love me. Do you love me, Anna? Answer me!"

"I love you," as if against her will, bashfully looking around, muttered the girl.

"You can't be with him. I'm made for you, and you are made for me." He unfolded a crumpled piece of paper on which he had scrawled a poem in Italian and started reading it to Anna.

People cheered, some applauded. Anna did not understand the verse's words and did not get what she should say, how to react. When he finished, she pleaded:

"Randall, please stand up. Don't attract the audience."

"You forget about the audience! They'll forget we exist in a second!"

At the end of the corridor, two burly, mustachioed guards were approaching.

"Randall, the security is coming! Stand up, I'm asking you! What do you want from me?" Tears flowed from her eyes. "I don't know what you want!"

"Don't fly away, please! Be with me!"

"Randall," Anna finally managed to lift him. "It's not serious. I have a life, a job, and I need to get back home."

"It's all nonsense!" Randall shouted through the whistle of the surrounding men. "All this does not matter. You have nothing in Mining-Great! You can't fly away and leave me alone! I can't be without you. I just can't stand it!"

His shoulders began to shake with sobs, and he covered his face with his hands.

"Randall." Anna felt a physical pain to look at him, and she hugged him.

"I do love you, Anna." He gazed her in the eyes. "And I know it now. I was such a fool. I lost you, and only this Teo got me to understand that you are everything to me, and I will never give you to him! Please don't fly away. We'll be together."

The guards stopped to ask what the commotion was. Two ladies enthusiastically described the story unfolding before the eyes of the onlookers, eventually making the guards allies of the spectacle.

"Randall, please don't cry." Anna herself cried, wiping his tears, and he wiped hers.

"I understand all now. I understand everything," he muttered. "Please stay... You can't leave"

Teo came back into the circle, and at the same moment, the speakers began to call for the passengers on Anna's flight to board.

"The concert is over, Randall!" Teo snapped. "Anna, you have a flight to catch."

Without answering, Randall grabbed Anna and begged again that she would not fly, assuring her of his love. Anna wept and stood like a statue in his arms.

She looked at Teo. There was so much shame and pain in his eyes, so much frustration and anger that no words were needed to understand what he felt at the moment.

She looked back at Randall. His tear-stained eyes expressed love and a kind of primal fear. She swallowed, glancing back at Teo.

"Randall, I have to go," she gasped, searching Teo's eyes for a reaction, but when she saw nothing, she looked back at Randall, whose eyes were filled with terror.

"You can't, you can't fly away!" he clutched his head.

"Randall, let me go, please," Anna repeated.

Randall looked her straight in the eye, trying to explain her decision to himself.

"Are you leaving me?"

"Randall"

"Are you leaving me?"

"She's got a plane, Randall." Teo snatched the girl's hand from Randall's grasp. "Go home."

Randall froze, staring at Anna. He couldn't believe it. He was so sure that his confession would change everything. The pain shot through him.

Teo was dragging Anna away, making his way through the staring crowd and making endless comments. Anna looked only at Randall, but continued walking with Teo.

Randall stood crying. He watched her go. When he realized she would not break away from Teo and run to him, he turned and walked down the hall without looking back.

"Randall!" Anna cried.

He didn't hear her. But she didn't scream for him to hear, because she didn't try to run after him. She was holding Teo's hand...

Chapter 80

Teo walked with her to the very last gate. They were silent.

"I have to go," Anna said.

"Take care of yourself, Anna," Teo managed to choke out. It was evident that even this phrase was difficult for him.

"You too," she said, with equal tension. "And Ricardo and Leti?"

"They won't come," Teo said dryly. "I explained to them why. They didn't need to see it all."

Anna drooped, and tears ran down her cheeks. Teo wiped them away with a flick of his hand.

"Hurry up," he urged. "You don't want to miss your flight."

"I don't" confirmed the girl, choking with tears. "Goodbye to you, Teo."

"Goodbye, Anna."

They hugged, and Anna ran to the plane. Not because she was late, but because she was consumed with shame and guilt in front of this wonderful guy who stood looking after her with pain.

Chapter 81

She rode in a taxi, looking at Mining Great City with tear-stained eyes. The place remained the same. Billboards burned just as brightly. People were just as indifferent to each other's existence and ran about their business in just as much haste.

Her head ached unbearably. She had been crying inconsolably all through the flight. As soon as she entered her dusty apartment, she crashed on the bed and fell asleep.

It was nearly noon when she finally opened her eyes again. The sun flooded the room with bright light, and a breeze stirred the curtains in the half-open window. Anna stretched and looked sleepily around the room.

That's all. The adventure was over. She thought and stood up lazily.

On the bed, she discovered the forgotten-before-travel phone and frankly cursed. How many misfortunes could have been avoided if her forgetfulness had not played this cruel trick! She would have just taken the phone with her, and the whole course of events would have turned out differently. But it was pointless to cherish the thought now. It had happened as it had happened. Anna believed in fate.

While the phone was charging, she took a shower and, for not having food in the house, went down to the coffee shop on the first floor of her house to buy a fresh espresso with a couple of sandwiches.

Her mood was unpredictable. She cried again, then rejoiced that she was finally home and seemed to forget about the events of the day before. The brain itself had not yet decided how to react to all this.

As soon as she turned on her phone and computer, Anna began reading her work e-mails. She found that her workplace was still fixed, but her boss was furious and would have fired her long ago if she had not been such a high-class teacher.

Smiling maliciously that she was getting away with it, Anna began to write a lengthy explanatory letter with many touching details without mentioning her real adventures. Lying was obviously bad, but keeping the job with its generous salary was far more critical, especially now. So, Anna, ignoring calls of heaven to repent, continued scribbling and promised tomorrow to show up at work and do best in the triple regime. She would take leadership, manage Olympiads, and whatever needed to be back in the boss's good graces.

Reassured that she was not unemployed and could breathe freely, she picked up the phone. Her hands began to tremble. She expected at least abusive messages from Randall or Teo, a bunch of angry texts from friends and acquaintances, and at least a million messages from Mark.

But her expectations were not met…

Chapter 82

There was nothing from Randall. Nothing at all. No messages, no missed calls. Nothing.

Only the realization of this brought a fresh wave of tears to Anna. He was not online for two days, according to the messenger. Now he was off, and panic engulfed her. She texted him, asking him where he was and how he was, and begging him to answer.

One missed call and one message came from Teo: *"Did you make it?"* She wrote that the flight went well, she was at home and not fired.

Indeed, from Mark was if not a million, then a good dozen messages. He wondered if she'd flown to Milan, where she was, why she wasn't answering, what was going on, how and when she'd finally get back to Mining, and if he should call the police.

Without a moment's hesitation, Anna dialed Mark's number. But a girl, whose voice Anna immediately recalled, picked up the phone.

"Well?" the lady wondered in a provocative tone.

"I need to talk to Mark. My name is Anna. I'm an old friend of his. Um… I flew back from Milan."

"And?"

"And I need to talk to him!" Anna said and swore under her breath, shocked by the girl's haughty tone.

"Mark isn't home," the girl said irritably.

"Where is he?"

"Left."

"Where?"

"What do you care?"

"Oh, come on!" Anna shouted. "Are you that insecure that you would pour water for half an hour to get rid of me as if it would help to keep Mark under your skirt?"

They hung up.

"What a sheep!" Anna reacted loudly. "I'll talk to him anyway. Where had he found her?"

Anna began to copy and paste messages to all her friends who worried about her, telling her how she liked Milan, that she had forgotten her phone at home, that everything was fine and how thrilled she was, and that life was beautiful. Universal messages to calm down and cheer up.

Then she telephoned her mother, and after a half-hour's tirade of reproaches, chatted with her for three and a half hours more, telling her the details of her journey.

Elena *ooh*-ed and *aah*-ed, commented and joked, and Anna felt infinitely calm at heart that she was at home. That she could again hear her mother's voice, that tomorrow she would begin her pleasant working days, hoping that fate, in which she so believed, would put everything in its place.

Chapter 83

No matter how many times Anna called, no matter how much she wrote, there was no way she could reach Randall. She was going insane from suffering, praying that Randall would take pity on her and pick up the phone at last.

She bombarded Bernardo with messages. He only answered once, saying that Randall had gone to China alone, without him. They had a big fight about it because Bernardo had a job to do. Randall didn't want to wait until his friend's vacation and left in a hurry, burning bridges behind him.

Though Teo wrote, the messages were cold. He answered dryly and distantly, as if he were a bot. The sentences were scored, that everything was fine, work was fine, and the music was okay. But there was nothing in these words.

Anna believed that she had hurt him so much that he was just being polite and forcing himself to keep in touch with her. Only respectful manners prevented him from sending her away and telling her what garbage of a person she was to him. However, Anna continued to write to him every day, and he answered, with long delays, making her check the phone several times a day in vain.

At the end of the week, the phone rang, and Anna, running out of the bathroom wet, rushed to answer, believing it was Randall or Teo.

But it was Mark.

Seeing his name on the screen, Anna hastily wiped her face and hands with a towel and answered:

"Mark?"

"Anna!" a familiar voice said. "Anna!"

"Mark! Hi!" She smiled as she continued drying herself. "Your girlfriend is annoying."

They laughed.

"Why, thank you! I just found out—in a fight, by the way—that you called me a week ago."

"Oh," Anna snorted, putting on her robe. "Why don't I look surprised."

"Where are you? How are you?"

"I returned to the capital. All is good! Back to work!"

"You weren't fired?"

"No!"

"Great!" Mark laughed, pleased to hear her voice again.

"Where are you? Can we meet tonight? I have so much to tell you!"

"Emm. No, it won't work! I'm in London!"

"You what?"

"I'm in London!" he repeated proudly. "I moved!"

"Why didn't you tell me? Ah, yes." Anna slapped her forehead. "Wait, you moved??"

"Oh, yes! I was promoted and offered a job with the British dep of my company, and I accepted it!"

"That's great news, Mark!" the girl gasped in admiration. "But why did you bring that diva with you?"

"You mean Emily?" Mark laughed with a hit of scorn. "She's my secretary actually, and she's been transferred, too. She is a beneficial team member."

"Sure, she is."

"Don't be so grumpy! I suppose you and Randall are together now? You went after him like a rocket, and I'm sure you found him!"

"I did find him." Anna's eyes filled with tears, and all desire to tell Mark the details immediately disappeared. "Well, I thought we'd go out one evening and have a chat."

"There! Life is crazy, huh?" Mark retorted. "I'm sure we'll see each other again. I have found you again, my dear Anna! You're back in touch!"

"Yes, of course." She smiled. "Wow, London! Mark, you're so cool! I dream of London!"

"Do come!"
"I will, one day!"
Emilia's voice was heard in the background.
"Okay, let's talk later! Okay?" Mark asked timidly.
"Of course," Anna said, and they hung up.
London!...
Had she lost even a friend forever?

Chapter 84

But they did not have a chance to talk again for a very long time. Routine life affairs again became a priority. Anna delved into a career and a new goal- to take a leading position in the educational institution.

For this, she took all sorts of courses, training, participated in the teachers' circle activities, and made new useful business acquaintances at conferences and forums. She intended to overthrow the head of the school and sit on her "iron" throne.

These new errands have become another panacea from obsessive thoughts about her love triangle, which has acquired the character of an enigma, overgrown with mysteries and confusion.

Anna still tried to find Randall, but as none of her attempts were successful, she gave up at one point. It was apparent he was avoiding her, and she decided that one day he would come and reconnect with her, if that was meant to be, and then fate would open her cards to their relationship.

She was still angry and tormented by the thoughts of him in bed with other girls, and sometimes it even helped her live every day apart from Randall.

Far more confusing was Teo. Though in touch, he seemed to be farther away than where Randall was hiding. His messages were even more seldom now. Even if they corresponded in the context of "boyfriend and girlfriend," it was so far from the truth. Teo wanted to be always busy performing, traveling and touring. He was planning to move to Sweden and talked to Anna like you speak to people in the streets— politely, tactfully, and... indifferently.

Such changes could not but hurt even more. Upset Anna regularly wrote to him, hoping for attention, messages, video chats, and requests to see him again and fix everything. She apologized endlessly, not knowing in her heart why she was running after Teo at all, more driven by feminine possessiveness than common sense or feeling. Her messages were often either unanswered, or he sent *"It's Okay"* and *"Don't think about anything."*

So, when she found herself alone and forsaken again, confused and lost, she plunged headlong into pursuing money. And she did it well again.

Chapter 85

"Miss Ryans, come in and sit down," the director pointed to an empty seat in the office.

Hesitating a moment, Anna sat down and cleared her throat:

"Why did you call me, Ma'am?"

"Miss Ryans," the woman began again.

"Anna."

"Anna. I've heard rumors that you have great ambitions, and I think the Principal's chair is very attractive to you and…" She cleared her throat, too. "You have far-reaching plans. Right?"

Anna didn't know what to say, but the head teacher went on,

"I would like to tell you that if you knew what a huge responsibility it is and what moments you need to keep under control, you would not aim at this place so… fiercely."

"Ma'am, I"

"But I understand. Young, ambitious, intelligent… you want to reach some heights. I understand all this. But I still cannot allow you to carry out what you have planned. I'm not giving up the Principal's chair. Over my dead body."

"I think such extremes are unnecessary," Anna smiled and added, "but the inauguration of the new directorship is entirely up to the parents and faculty of the School 678, and here I suppose…"

"Anna!" suddenly blurted out Mrs. Treethers. "How can you so coolly step on people and go ahead for dethroning me from a position that is the passion of my entire life! Is nothing sacred to you?"

"You're exaggerating, Ma'am," Anna frowned.

"What? Look what you're doing? Do you think I don't have eyes and ears? With your victories and contributions, you win over people before voting."

"That sounds fair."

"This is cruel. Anna, is it so important for you to become the principal of this school?"

"Career is important to me, Mrs. Treethers, and I'm getting it straight, in the normal and obvious way. I don't see the point of your claims." Anna shrugged, annoyed.

"And the human attitude? Did we not sit with you at the teachers' gatherings, talking about dreams and careers? Don't you remember me telling you my way to that chair?"

"Ma'am."

"Miss Ryans. Anna. I speak to you now not as a colleague but as a friend. Please, Anna. Back off."

"Ma'am. Being a teacher, a principal, or something else is not enough for me. It is a step in a ladder."

Mrs. Treethers' eyes glistened with tears, and Anna looked away, not to embarrass her even more.

"I can transfer you to our London school branch. We have a partnership with a British institution, and I will arrange your transfer as a teacher. But this is a temporary matter. Miss Ryans, step back."

"Perfect," Anna said suddenly.

"Excuse me?"

"Great!"

"Are you serious?" the director froze in her movements.

"I like your offer of the transfer. I accept it, waiting for sponsorship in the visa and registration of all necessary documents for my legal residence and teaching at this school."

"Will you back down at the election?" the Director asked.

"I will."

Mrs. Treethers, not believing her ears, went up to Anna to shake her hand.

"I can't believe it. Thanks. Are you sure you're ready to move?"

"Yes. I need a change of scenery." Anna swallowed. "Can I go now?"

"O-of course. Thank you again."

Anna walked out the door, and Mrs. Treethers gave way to tears of relief.

Chapter 86

The first thing Anna did when she left the principal's office was to text Mark. Fate was giving them a chance to meet again because she was coming to London soon.

They corresponded now by email because of Mark's girlfriend's long nose and his constant employment, and only in a friendly and polite way.

The expectation of receiving a reply by letter seemed to be even worse than continually checking the messenger. Anna nervously put the phone in her pocket, knowing that the news response would not come soon.

And indeed, the answer tarred as much as a week. Anna had already forgotten about it. Life events did not give her a chance to writhing with boredom. She was passing her driving license exams, studying in absentia on the faculty of philosophy, walking six dogs of her neighbor out of sincere kindness and for the sake of squeezing several minutes for rest while they perform their canine affairs.

The answer from Mark came late at night. With her feet up against the wall, Anna was reading "Pride and Prejudice," sighing and asking the Universe why it had not given her the same Mr. Darcy. As soon as the notification rang, Anna read it and beamed. The smile slowly but surely faded from her face, as she was reading the e-mail:

"Hi, Anna! Wow, that's news! What does it all mean? Meteoric career growth? You didn't write any details! What is the job? How? Where? I need all the details! And I hurry to share news, too! On October 12, I have a wedding! I was planning on writing to you, but you beat me to it. It doesn't matter, though. Emilia and I invite you to the ceremony, and you have no right to refuse! The colorful invitation should be in your mailbox any day now, and I hope you don't let me down and come. I need your support! Who would have thought! I'm getting married, hehe! Text me. I'll nervously check my mail every day. Kisses, Mark."

"Who would have thought..." Anna murmured.

She stared at the screen, trying to understand her emotions. What was this, a joke of fate? A wedding? In a flash, she remembered all the dreams, all the memories about her relationship with Mark. Her dreams of marriage with him, children, a happy family life.

She thought nothing about Mark could hurt her. In his time, he extinguished her love effectually, so she was at her ease, and it would be silly to react to anything at all. And yet, she felt pain. Hurt feelings, resentment. Spite. Even some hatred for him and his lady at that moment.

She just sat there, aware of what she was feeling.

"No way. Just unbelievable!" she barked and began to type a brief reply.

"Mark! Congratulations! Of course, I'll be at your party! About work and other things, we will talk upon my arrival, long to write. See you later, Anna."

"Unbelievable," Anna commented rather on her own condition.

She didn't want to read or do anything else that day.

Chapter 87

She had never seen anything more beautiful than London. Now, she was sitting in a London cab, craning her neck to look at the passing sights and taking pictures of everything.

It was a dream come true. It was the England she had drawn maps of as a little girl. Here were the English people, whose language she worshipped, running their errands. These were the places she'd read about in books. She was here! She was here! She was here!

Anna's face broke into a wide smile. She felt nothing but infinite happiness.

The taxi stopped at the campus gate of Anna's future place of work an hour later. The school was huge, in several buildings. Anna was quickly met and shown to the dormitory for teachers.

Although it was possible to rent an apartment without problems, Anna still wanted to immerse herself in academic life, make friends with colleagues, and quickly join society. Otherwise, she would never have shown such friendliness, but this was Great Britain, baby! She wanted to know and be a friend to everyone. Logic can be immediately disabled when a child's dream becomes a reality.

Anna and Mark agreed to meet the next day at The National Gallery square, which was always full of people, absorbing even the noise of the endless stream of cars with their hubbub.

Anna shifted nervously from one foot to the other, afraid that Mark had forgotten the meeting. He didn't answer her calls or texts. As she was waiting, she wondered why he was so late.

Mark came into view twenty minutes later and was not alone. None other than the bride-to-be herself accompanied him. As he was approaching, he looked guiltily into Anna's eyes.

"I'm sorry, Anna. I know we're late, but the traffic is terrible. We got stuck in a traffic jam for an hour and a half getting here from the suburbs."

"It's okay!" Anna said, embarrassed that Mark had come with a fiancee.

"Please, let me introduce you Emilia, my future wife," Mark hurried on, as if reading her gaze. "Emily, this is Anna, my school friend."

Emilia was a stunning woman. Tall, with a wasp waist, she was dressed stylishly, in the latest fashion. Her blonde hair was neatly styled in waves, and her minimal make-up betrayed a sophisticated taste. She smelled of expensive perfume even from a distance, and undoubtedly she made an instant positive impression even among those who should not like her at all.

However, all this impression of delight at how gorgeous beauty looks were spoiled the second she opened her mouth. A gratuitous haughtiness and an apparent hostility that Emily, even out of politeness, did not intend to conceal, at once built a wall the size of the Great Wall of China between them.

Anna hadn't planned to be best friends with someone who took her place if life turned out differently. But for the sake of decency, she was always ready to smile and be friendly when the situation demanded it.

Here, when Emilia did not even bother to pretend that she was pleased to meet her. Anna was unpleasantly embarrassed and already foresaw that they would enjoy a tedious and unpleasant walk in a "third wheel" style. Anna had assumed that Mark must have a good reason for bringing Emily with him, but that didn't help at all to dispel the impending bad mood.

"We know each other," Emilia grunted in response to the performance.

"Not personally," Anna corrected.

Mark, glancing nervously at the two women, hastened to suggest.

"Okay, ladies. Shall we go to a cafe? There's a great place across the street. Although even on the way there, we'll come across a lot of great eateries."

"Take us to a proper restaurant, Mark." Emily shook her head. "You have a visitor, after all. It's no good taking her to a diner."

Anna raised an eyebrow.

"Oh, that is quite all right. I have half an hour, I am very…"

"Of course, I'm sorry," Mark apologized. "Then we'll steer to the left, and it won't take long. There is a great Italian restaurant with equally great Italian cuisine very close by."

So the company went to look for the place recommended by Mark.

Chapter 88

A few minutes later, they were sitting at a beautiful table, very similar to the interior of one of those that Anna met in Milan.

She sighed sadly and rechecked her phone. While Mark did all the ordering, she decided to write a message to Teo and try her luck again.

She had completely lost all thread of understanding of the relationship in which she either was or was not. There was no point in asking, but the girl's heart was not made of stone. She missed Teo, the way he talked, the way he drove, the way he had confidence in himself.

Hesitating for a moment, she texted, *"I miss you so much, Teo. Please write back."*

Surprisingly, Teo answered immediately:

"And I miss you very much, Anna. But the choice was not mine."

Resentment and disappointment surged through her. Emilia saw the tears in Anna's eyes and suggested:

"Listen, Markie. Your friend looks like she's going to cry. I think you should do something, talk to her, or whatever. Because I have nothing to say to her."

Mark turned from his conversation with the waiter and looked anxiously at Anna, who lowered her eyes in shame and anger, trying to wipe away the treacherous tears with her sleeve.

"Emilia, we'll leave you for a little while, okay? We'll be back shortly."

"Pf," Emilia reacted.

Mark took Anna's arm and led her out onto the restaurant's balcony, closing the door behind them.

"What's the matter with you? What is it?" he asked anxiously.

"I-I don't know what's the matter with me!" Anna shook her head, no longer holding back her tears. "But I'm fine."

"Anna," Mark insisted. "I know you better than you do. What's wrong?"

"I don't know, Mark!" Anna exclaimed. "I don't know what's going on in my life. I got into a love triangle and got out of it in the end, absolutely alone."

"What are you talking about?"

"Oh, Mark! Do you hear that?"

"What? What do you mean?"

"The song?"

"What?"

"The song, Mark! The song is on! Do you hear it?"

"Yes, of course, I do. So what?"

"This is Iris from Sleeping with Sirens. He played me this song the very first time we saw each other on video."

"Who?"

Anna wept bitterly, and Mark asked irritably:

"Anna, you speak in riddles, and I do not like it. Tell me who you're talking about."

"Teo. I'm talking about Teo. The guy I went to on my second trip to Milan to get back at Randall for cheating on me."

"Ah, yes, your silly revenge. Did you succeed?"

"Managed. Randall suddenly said he loved me."

"He's thirteen years old, just like you. You two deserve each other."

"But I rejected him."

"What?"

"He wanted us to be together, but I turned him down."

"You decided to stay with the other one?"

"With the other one, I believe it is all over, too"

"Why? He left you?"

"I suppose so… But he doesn't say that. He's mad at me for the way I treated him, and God knows I understand it all."

"So apologize to him. What's stopping you? Does he love you?"

"I don't know, Mark. He said he loved me, and now he doesn't even want to keep in touch"

"Being angry and not loving are two different things. What do you want, Anna? Who do you love?"

"I want to be with Teo... He's a great guy, and I'm sure I just need more time to love him. I tried, but"

Mark licked his lips. In the gesture, Anna even read a particular disgust that Mark felt for their conversation.

"So, you're in no hurry to bring back the second guy," he concluded.

"Teo is gorgeous, he's unique, he's amazing... but I don't love him."

"You love Randall." He opened the door and called to a passing waiter.

"I love Randall," Anna said, almost in a whisper.

Mark fell silent.

Chapter 89

A minute later, a waiter came out on the balcony with a glass of vodka, which Mark, to the surprise of both Anna and the waiter, drained for a split second without wincing.

"It will be much easier for me to listen to all your nonsense now, Anna." He smiled, motioning the waiter to repeat.

"What do I do now?" Anna sighed, wiping away her tears with her already wet shirt sleeve.

"Go to your Randall and be happy. What else is there to do?"

"Randall doesn't want to know me. He's gone, doesn't even want to talk. I never found a way to talk to him after my trip to Milan. He severed all contact with me."

"Delirium," Mark stated, draining another glass of vodka the waiter had brought.

Anna raised an eyebrow.

"Why are you drinking?"

Mark signaled again for more vodka and turned to Anna:

"I'm getting married soon, remember?"

"I remember, but"

"I'm so happy," Mark said with a sarcastic note in his voice. "Me and Emilia. Aren't we a match made in heaven?"

Anna frowned.

"There!" Mark snapped his fingers. The shots were beginning to get into his head. "And I think so, too!"

"What?"

"There!" he opened the door ajar and gestured toward the table, where Emilia had been waiting for them. "My bride! My beautiful Emilia! Isn't she beautiful?"

"Very," Anna nodded suspiciously. "Mark, you're getting drunk, and I don't get why."

"No, I'm sober." Mark approached the girl. "But I still can't wrap my head around how you can suffer all this delirium, Anna. I can't get any of this into my head!"

"Mark"

"What are you doing here, anyway?"

"What?"

"Why did you come?"

"What?" Anna sat up." I have a job here!"

"Really? From all over the world, you chose exactly where I moved to poison my life?"

"What??"

"Do you think I'm a fool, Anna?"

"I'm sure you are!" cried the astonished girl.

"You came to torment me!"

"What are you saying?"

"You have come to drive me mad with your presence. You know that I love you and suffer for you, yet it is not enough for you. That's who you're taking revenge on, Anna! Here is your most insidious plan! You plan to ruin my whole life!"

"That's crazy, Mark! What thoughts you have in your head!" Anna covered her face with her hands in horror. "How can you think all this heresy?"

"I tried to live every day, killing the hope that one day you would forgive me and come back to me. I regret every day of my miserable life, the day I didn't dare to take you with me, but I was afraid. I was a coward. I didn't want to have what I dream about now. I dreaded the thought of marriage then, and every morning I think how beautiful my life would have been if you had been my wife instead of Emily. I"

"Mark!"

"I have prayed to God to turn back time, but it is impossible. I'm getting married to Emilia just because she's my last chance to touch the strings of your heart. Even if I don't feel anything for her, I"

"Mark!!" Anna cried again.

"I'll finish. You should know that."

"Mark! Stop talking! *Emilia's here!*"

Chapter 90

Mark turned around. In the door stood a dumbfounded waiter with a glass of vodka, and Emilia. She stood stock-still, the horror of what she had heard piercing her very being. They met eyes, and the next moment Emilia, turning over a tray with a glass of vodka, ran out. There were shouts and curses.

Mark didn't run after her. He drooped and sank heavily into the corner of the balcony between the railings.

Anna stood in utter shock. From the whole scene, she could not even move. Mark looked up and stared at her.

"I'll tell you something, Anna. The day we called, and I invited you over for vacation, I bought a wedding ring. You didn't let me finish what I was to tell you on the phone, but I was going to propose to you. I had hoped so much that you would agree to come, and I would ask your forgiveness for everything—for leaving you so meanly and cowardly, for chasing empty things instead of looking forward to the future with you. I prayed to God that you would forgive me. I could make things right and beg you to marry me, so I would never lose you again. But, look at how things turned out… You came, but not to me, fell in love again, but not with me, and I got so depressed. I was beside myself with jealousy and anger. So one night, when I was pretty drunk at work, I slept with Emilia. She stayed with me that night. In the morning, she saw a box with a ring on the table, and I proposed to her. I didn't care about anything."

He looked down again and was silent.

At that moment, Anna wished the earth would open and swallow her.

Chapter 91

Anna walked home in the pouring rain. The rain was merciless. It looked like heaven intended to wash the Earth from its endless sins. It poured on the streets and pavements, streaking every object in its way.

It was that rain—the water of revival and remorse, power and transformation. Everything buckled under the force of its flow.

Anna was watching a poor, drenched, middle-aged gentleman. To his misfortune, he had been caught in the middle of a downpour. He hurried home as fast as he could, his feet slithering, slipping, and sinking in the mud, but his expression betrayed the thought at home, he would find a dry bed and a hot supper, perhaps wife and children.

Anna ambled as if hoping that the water would wash away the whole day with all its words and events. She had left Mark alone on the balcony, calling him names in desperation, blaming him for all the troubles of her life and threatening that it was not him who should whine about the sad fate but her, because everything had gone downhill when he left her alone face to face with destiny. She accused him of being a weakling and a coward, of not fighting for them. That if he loved her, he would have never given up.

She regretted every word she uttered, but she couldn't stop herself at that moment. Mark listened with bowed head and guilty eyes full of tears. She had never seen him cry, never seen his face express so much pain.

She was walking down the street now, rewinding the conversation over and over, over and over. Mark had brought back in one night all the heart-rending memories and dreams that Anna had buried with a superhuman effort. Her cherished dreams of marriage, children, husband, and simple domestic happiness had been forcibly drawn from the depths of her heart, and pain had again pierced her whole being.

"Oh, Mark... How comes... Why are you..." The rain's noise swallowed her sentence.

The man ahead of Anna ran up to the porch of his house, met by his wife and two daughters, who immediately threw a huge towel over him and joyfully hugged him.

Chapter 92

Over the next few days, Anna deliberately turned off her phone because the drama in her life was off the charts. She took extra time to distract herself from obsessive thoughts and worries, stayed late at work, tried to eat out of the teachers' dorm, and returned only to go straight to bed and hurry back to work in the morning.

That's what happened today as well. She took on the Olympics event and the tea party for the occasion and had hundreds of copybooks to check. It was about 11 p.m., and a security guard, passing by, hinted that if she kept coming home at midnight, no one would believe she was a teacher but a representative of a different profession. Politely assessing the joke on three points out of ten, Anna built a semblance of smiles and started to collect things.

When she reached the teachers' campus, she flew up the stairs to the fifth floor and collapsed on the bed in the room.

In a couple of minutes, pebbles began to hit her window. Anna jumped up and opened it.

Beneath stood Mark with a huge bouquet and balloons in the form of hearts.

"Mark? What are you doing? It is a closed area!" Anna hissed from above.

"You haven't answered for a week. That's the only way I could find you!" Mark shouted back so that a dog barked somewhere near. "Look, I bought balloons. The saleswoman said that it is from them the lady's heart melts."

"Mark, don't shout like that. They'll hear us!"

"Let them hear!"

In several windows, a light came on, and sleepy voices were heard.

"I came to tell you," Mark went on, "that I'll never give up. I will fight for your heart every day until my last breath. From your life, I will go nowhere. I will be anyone for you. I don't care. But we both have to be whole, and without each other, it is impossible. You are everything for me, Anna. I never thought without your happiness, my own is impossible. I know you only wanted to love and be loved forever. I refused to admit to myself that I needed you. I owe you everything. We are bound in this forever. Everything else, all these people are a game. There are only you and I. I love you, Anna. So no, I will never give up the fight for you now. I realized all my mistakes!"

"Aww!" came the affectionate reactions of the gawkers from the windows.

"Mark" Anna could only say.

"I didn't come to pressure you. I only came to say that. And to give balloons. Because the saleswoman said that it is from the balloons, the lady's heart melts."

"Aww!" again exclaimed the colleagues. "Anna, forgive him! What had he done?" some asked. "Look at him, poor thing!" others commented. "You deserve it!" others grumbled.

Mark did not put Anna in an awkward position, waiting for a response. He only asked her to come down to receive the flowers, assuring her he would disappear at once.

Anna grabbed her cardigan and left the room. When she ran outside to Mark, everyone was cheering again, urging Anna to kiss him to make it look like a movie.

They stood looking into each other's eyes. Mark's eyes were full of sadness, questions, and… hope. Anna sighed.

"I'm sorry I said so many nasty things to you in the cafe. I just"

"But you were right," Mark stopped her. "You were right about everything. I *am* a coward and a weakling. But not now. I won't make those mistakes again. I won't lose you again."

"Mark, I"

"I don't expect you to tell me you love me, Anna. I know what you're going to say. I'm just asking you to give me a chance and time to prove to you that everything can be returned. I'm ready to wait for you all my life. I'll never back down."

Anna smiled sadly. He glanced into her eyes and repeated: "I'll never let you down again, Anna. I promise."
And he kept his promise.

Chapter 93

The next time Teo got back in touch, a few months had passed, and he had already moved to live in Sweden. Calling Anna late one night, he asked her to come back to him, that he could not forget her, that he tried to pay attention to other girls, but Anna did not go out of his head.

"Please come back to me, Anna."

"I can't, Teo. I'm in a relationship."

"I don't care. Leave him and be with me."

"I'm pregnant."

Randall also got in touch, but much later, when he returned to Italy from China after a year's absence. Bernardo persuaded him to contact Anna that it was impossible to live without a restored peace.

When they called, they talked on a friendly note.

Anna was already married.

Chapter 94

The last chapter, which is the first one as well.

"And no girlfriends!" she smirked, hearing her son's protests. "Well, darling, off you go. Thank you for paying me mind. I love you. Call at the slightest opportunity."

She finished a call and turned back to her beloved.

"Listen."

The husband looked inquiring.

"I am so, so happy." She pulled Mark into her arms and again looked in a window.

What fine weather...

... But IS IT FOREVER?...

Chapter 49(B)

The excluded additional chapter for those who paid attention to even the smallest details. Thank you so much for being such devoted readers of the novel. I hope you could match the pieces of the mosaic and understand so much more.

I took this chapter out and placed it at the end of the book for a reason, so you could understand that there is never one truth to the story. Unless you have witnessed something with your own eyes, you cannot know things for sure and have to act according to the facts you are told.

No matter what, I believe that the truth always comes out.

I hope you would be thrilled to read a bit more in-depth about some events from the story.

And from all my heart—thank you.

***

Teo's eyes burned with rage. He stormed out of the house, yelling to Ricardo to get in the car with him. The friend quickly put out the cigarette he had been puffing a few minutes calmly before and hurled questions at Teo, to which he received only an irritated snarl in response.

"I'll smear his pretty face on the door of his art-house!" Teo shouted as he started the engine.

"What is he doing? He said he was coming to pick her up at five-thirty! This is how brazen you have to be!"

"Hey, calm down!" Ri snapped at him." We'll sort it out now."

"Sort it out? Oh, no. You will keep me from going to jail for murder."

"Where's Anna?"

"Staying home."

"What did you do to her?"

Teo stopped the car abruptly and gazed at Ricardo.

"What did I do to her? What kind of question is this, Ri? Do you think I can hurt Anna? Can't you see that I love her?"

"I can see that! And I can see that she doesn't love you, and such stories are rare to end on a good note."

"I would never hurt her, no matter what." Teo slammed his fists on the steering wheel and started the car again. "She mocks me, but only because I let her. I can't help it."

Teo lowered his voice to a whisper.

"Because I love her. Even if she doesn't love me."

Ricardo sighed heavily. They spent the rest of the way to Randall's house in silence.

Teo parked on the next street and went straight to Randall's without waiting for Ricardo to finish his cigarette.

After a couple of knocks, the door opened, and Teo's fist landed on Randall's face.

"What in the world?" Randall roared, falling inside the house.

Teo fell on him with punches, and a fight ensued.

"I'm going to kill you right now, Randall!" Teo yelled, showering the guy with punches and getting punched in return.

"I've been waiting for this moment!" Randall shouted. His eyes were bloodshot. He was hitting his opponent with full force, rolling with him all over the living room.

There was a clink of falling China, vases, and figurines breaking into small fragments. As the guys threw each other in different directions, pieces of furniture, paintings, photos on the walls, and all sorts of decorative elements have been shattering.

"I can't understand," Randall blurted out, taking a moment to catch his breath between two broken floor vases, "how do you not hate being with someone who dreams of me?"

"Come down from heaven to earth!" Teo barked at him. "Anna dreams not of you but of love, which she drew in her head and mistakenly assumed that you can make this dream come true. You can't do that. You don't know what love is."

With that, Teo bumped into Randall again and slapped him across the face.

"You're desperate!" Randall grinned. "I'm sorry for you. Came here to fight because you don't know what you have to do to get me out of Anna's heart."

"I came here to fight because you don't know what you can do to keep Anna from being a poor confused girl, a toy in your hands. It's so convenient always to have one who comes running to you when the other switches the brain on. And you can't lose a fan club. It's dangerous for your self-esteem. You have a lot of chicks like her, but the situation with Anna makes you so angry because Anna is with me now."

"That's right. With you. Let it be with anyone but you. You sing your snotty love songs and stuff girls with drugs."

"How dare you!" Teo leaped at Randall and knocked him to the floor, beating him in a rage.

There were no more opportunities for constructive, or indeed, any dialogue.

Ricardo, knowing that he should not be in a hurry but should only arrive at the end—either to spread the roosters apart, or help Teo with the corpse—calmly finished his other cigarette and went to Randall's house, only when there was an unusual noise from inside.

As soon as he entered the living room, he saw them fighting and hurried to separate them. By his second's objective assessment, Randall was losing consciousness, and Teo was trying to strangle him. Ricardo hoicked Teo back and spent the next couple of minutes making sure that his friend would not attack Randall with the desire to finish him off but rather aim for the exit.

It gave Randall time to catch his breath. Coughing and rubbing his neck, he muttered after them:

"She will never love you. Not because she loves me. But because all your weaknesses can be sensed a mile away. You make yourself seem strong, but you can't fool women. She feels everything, Teo. You're weak."

Teo made another attempt to break out of Ricardo's grip and strangle Randall, but the lad himself suddenly jumped on both guys and began handing out punches with an animal growl. Ricardo and Teo held Randall back the best they could because two against one would have been a low, dishonest fight. But Randall grew insane and threw punches and insults simultaneously, and Teo, with one movement, sharply blocked him and broke his striking arm.

Randall howled in pain and fell to the floor.

"You are pathetic!" he yelled to Teo and Ricardo as they were heading out.

In the living room, next to the door, Randall's phone was ringing on the floor. Teo picked it up and darted a glance at the screen.

It was *"Liz pretty from the bar."* Teo snorted and threw the phone against the wall.

"*You* are pathetic!" he shouted back to Randall and followed Ricardo out of the house.

***

The door slammed. Dropping the books, Anna ran down the stairs.

Teo and Ricardo spoke sharply in Italian.

"Teo!" Anna cried out. "What did you do, Teo??"

"Calm down. Your lover is safe and sound, Anna. He was not at home. He was nowhere to be found, actually."

About the Author

Yana Stevelork has always been passionate about writing, reading, and linguistics. Words have sacred meaning to her, and whenever she is not writing, she is learning the languages.

In her free time, she enjoys painting the surroundings while sauntering down the streets and creating endless worlds in her imagination.

www.ingramcontent.com/pod-product-compliance
Lightning Source LLC
LaVergne TN
LVHW041659070526
838199LV00045B/1123